I0761090

Frankie

Frankie

J. M. GUTSCH
AND
MAXIM LEO

Translated by Sharon Howe

DOUBLEDAY CANADA

PUBLISHED IN 2025 BY DOUBLEDAY CANADA

First published in the United Kingdom by Penguin Michael Joseph,
a division of Penguin Random House UK, London.

Doubleday Canada, an imprint of Penguin Random House Canada Limited,
320 Front Street West, Suite 1400, Toronto, Ontario, M5V 3B6, Canada
penguinrandomhouse.ca

The authorized representative in the EU for product safety and compliance is
Penguin Random House Ireland, Morrison Chambers, 32 Nassau Street,
Dublin, D02 YH68, Ireland, https://eu-contact.penguin.ie

Library and Archives Canada Cataloguing in Publication
Title: Frankie / J.M. Gutsch and Maxim Leo.
Other titles: Frankie. English
Names: Gutsch, Jochen-Martin, 1971- author | Leo, Maxim, 1970- author
Description: Translation of: Frankie. | In English, translated from the German.
Identifiers: Canadiana (print) 20250151685 | Canadiana (ebook) 20250151715 | ISBN 9780385701006
(hardcover) | ISBN 9780385701013 (EPUB)
Subjects: LCGFT: Novels.
Classification: LCC PT2707.U89 F7313 2025 | DDC 833/.92—dc23

Cover design by Kate Sinclair
Cover illustration based on an image by Iryna Auhustsinovich / Stocksy
Typeset by Falcon Oast Graphic Art Ltd

Printed in Canada

2 4 6 8 9 7 5 3 1

'What makes life so difficult?'

'People?'

An Affair to Remember

1. The Piece of String

I've been told you should always tell a story starting from the top. Or the beginning. But being a tomcat, I know nothing of tops or beginnings. Humans have all sorts of rules for how life should be. They'll order you about: 'do this, do that!' Sounds like a bit of a drag if you ask me. Too much like hard work, and hard work has never been my style. So I'm going to start any old where. It might just happen to be the top. Or the beginning.

It was the nice time of the year, and by that I mean the time when the evenings were warm and long and bees were buzzing in the lime trees. On one of those evenings, I decided to pop over to the Professor's. I'll tell you more about who the Professor is later: he doesn't make an appearance in our story for a while.

There I am, trotting along the Big Road that goes through the middle of the village. Past the lake, where the grass is high and I stop to eat a few grasshoppers. D'you know what I love about grasshoppers? They never complain when you eat them. Not like birds. Birds always make such a fuss. 'Ooh, don't eat me! I'm a mother, with ten babies in the nest!' they'll cry. So over the top. But it catches me out every time, old Muggins that I am. Really puts a dampener on your appetite. I'm left standing there with a mouthful of bird and – for a moment or two – a guilty conscience. And then the moment passes.

So on I go, past the village church, past the ramshackle birdhouse, past Fatty Heinz the Rottweiler's vile-smelling pee, past two compost heaps with nothing decent to eat on them, not even anything halfway decent. Just coffee grounds, eggshells, potato skins and apple peel. Humans, let me clue you in on a little secret. A compost heap made of nothing but peel makes you look cheap. On I go, past the big sandhill just before the wood begins and beyond which the world ends. I'm in good spirits, strutting along all cool and calm in the evening light. When I get to an old wooden fence, I slip through it and into the garden of the Deserted House. Everyone calls it the *Deserted House* because one day the people from the city who used to spend every summer there stopped coming.

All the windows are closed and the curtains drawn, and in winter the wind howls all around the house. Fatty Heinz (who's a certified moron, by the way) has heard the noise and thinks there's a pack of werewolves living there.

But something odd is afoot: I'm nearly past the Deserted House when I spot a man *inside* the house! Utterly spooked, I crouch behind a bush and hide. Talk about getting the heebie-jeebies! While I'm sat there, another thought crosses my mind: *Well, shit, Frankie. What happens now?*

I'm tempted to run straight back home and tell everyone I know the big news. But I also know the inevitable inquisition that would follow. 'What did the man look like, Frankie?', 'What did the man smell like, Frankie?', 'What's the food like at the man's place, Frankie?', 'Are you quite sure it wasn't a werewolf, Frankie?'

When an empty house is suddenly no longer empty, all sorts of questions bubble to the surface. Everyone wants to know more. And if you can't give them any details, you're the one who ends up looking stupid.

So I do what any tomcat worth his salt would do in these trying circumstances: I stay put, and I peer out from behind my bush.

Listening.

Looking.

Listening.

Looking.

(This went on for quite a while so I'm giving you the abridged version.)

Listening.

Looking.

And so on.

Then I creep closer – ever so softly – and when I'm within a few cats' tails of the big window I peer in and begin to gather clues.

Clue 1: There really *is* a man in there.

Clue 2: The man is standing on a chair.

Clue 3: There is a string hanging from the ceiling.

Clue 4: The man is wearing the string around his neck.

Clue 5: Further to Clue 4, the string is very thick.

No kidding, I've never seen such a whopper! I'm a

string connoisseur, you see, so I would know. And I'm telling you, this string was the bee's knees. When I lived with Old Mrs Berkowitz, we used to play with the stuff nearly every day. There was never a human on the end of it though, only a mouse sometimes – not a real one of course, just a woolly one. (Humans seem to think we cats are fooled by this, but for the record, we're not. We're not stupid.)

So when I see this beauty, I'm suddenly reminded of Old Mrs Berkowitz and the best time of my life . . . which sadly didn't last very long. It ended when, one day, Old Mrs Berkowitz lay down abruptly in the garden and two men arrived soon after – all in white – bundling her into a big car with flashing lights on the roof. I never saw her again after that.

Remembering all this gives me a funny sort of ache in my heart, and I'm tempted to call out to the man: 'Hey, you there! Playing with the string! That's a beautiful specimen! Can I play too?'

But I know I mustn't say anything.

Instead, I pluck up all my courage, jump on to the window ledge and peer inside. The man is standing on a chair with the string around his neck. Then he sees me, and looks surprised. He certainly doesn't seem pleased to see me. He actually seems rather angry. He opens and closes his mouth like a carp, saying something to me, but I can't make out what because – to state the obvious – he's behind the windowpane and I'm in front of it.

So instead, I start my blinking routine. Humans, here's another hot tip: when a cat blinks, it's a bit like smiling.

Blinking translates as: *hey there, amigo, everything's cool. I'm good, you're good. Wassup?* I'm blinking manically at the man through the window, but he seems to have about as many brain cells to rub together as Fatty Heinz, and doesn't catch my drift.

Instead, he waves his arms around in my general direction. I raise my right paw to say: *Hey, no worries! I understand.* I know better than most that it's easy to get carried away when you're playing with string. Though to be honest, the whole arm-waving business looked a little odd. I lick my privates for a bit to calm my frazzled nerves.

What happens next happens quickly. The man lets go of his string and jumps down off the chair, and within seconds, the door of the Deserted House flies open. He reaches for an object of some sort and hurls it at me. I skedaddle, but I'm in shock and my legs go all wobbly! I see a shadow approaching. Something's chasing after me and pounces on my head.

I don't remember anything else after that.

The next thing I know, the wind is whispering something to me. I strain to listen but can't make out what it's saying. I'm lying on the lawn in front of the Deserted House, worn out and motionless. I can hardly open my eyes. And the wind keeps on whispering, until I realize it isn't the wind after all. It's the man bending over and speaking to me. He nudges me with his foot, as if I'm a dead rat or something. 'You all right?' he asks. It's a rather stupid question if you ask me, seeing as how I'm very obviously *not* all right. I'm so exhausted that I fall right back to sleep.

When I come around again, I don't know where I am at first. I'm feeling rather woozy, and I peer around warily. Then I spot that marvellous string hanging from the ceiling, and my memories come flooding back to me. I'm *inside* the Deserted House! On a couch, to be precise, with a newspaper spread under me and the man now sitting opposite me in an armchair. He's holding a tiny telephone to his ear and is talking agitatedly to someone. I might have no idea *who* he's talking to, but I can tell you *what* he's talking about: yours truly.

Speaking into his telephone, the man says: 'I've got a dead cat here. Can you drop by? Yes, she really does look very dead. But look, I'm no vet, so that's why I'm calling. No, she's not my cat! I've no clue who it belongs to. What does the cat look like? What does that matter? It's a cat! Grey tabby coat, a bit mangy, with a lump out of one of its ears. No, I don't know how she died! Yes, I found the cat in my garden. Listen . . . OK, my address is . . . No, the cat . . .'

'Ttmmcctt!' I slur.

That was obviously a bad move. The Professor (who you'll meet later) is always saying I should be a little savvier – more tactful – or else I'll get myself into trouble one day.

But I was feeling pretty peeved, to be honest. First, I'm nearly clobbered to death. Then, to add insult to injury, this human keeps referring to me as a molly, even though I'm clearly a full-blooded tomcat!

‘What?’ the man asks.

‘Ttmmcctt!’

My Humanish is a bit . . . *sluggish*? And whatever whacked my head has made me dizzy. I have to keep repeating the words over and over until finally I can say with perfect diction: ‘I’m a tomcat!’

The man gawps at me as if I’m some kind of alien.

In my experience, whenever a cat decides to speak, humans behave downright bizarrely. Every. Time. Without fail! That’s why I gave up speaking long ago. The last time I spoke was outside the village shop. Something fell out of this woman’s shopping bag, so I say, ‘Excuse me, madam, but are those your Hoover bags?’

And lo and behold, she took off screaming. I could hear her yelling all the way down the high street! Not the brightest spark, it seems.

Humanish is dead easy. The first word I ever said was *snow*. And then I picked up more and more. A lot of the animals at the shelter spoke Humanish, and so did Old Mrs Berkowitz, and so did her TV.

I used to speak Humanish better than Cattish.

Nowadays I can speak about ten languages. Which isn’t all that many. The Professor speaks twenty-seven, even Goatish, which almost no one speaks. Other than goats of course. As a cat, you’re basically stuffed if you don’t speak any foreign languages. Do you want to know why? Biodiversity! Wherever you go, you come across other animals with other languages, and not all animals are the kind you can eat, or tear in two, or torment to death. So you have to resort to talking. It wasn't my idea: that's just the way it is. Say I'm walking through the woods for instance. There's this giant owl there who spends his whole day sitting on a branch, with a face like a wet weekend. So I always like to strike up some friendly conversation in Owlish to lighten the mood.

'Hey, Owl. How's it hanging?'

'Mustn't grumble,' Owl replies.

'Yeah, mustn't grumble.' I nod. 'Keep your pecker up!'

'Right you are, Frankie!'

And just like that, you can exchange pleasantries with all sorts of animals, even with an owl who does nothing but sit on a branch all day long. Humans are the only ones who lose their minds when I speak.

Anyway, back to the man in the Deserted House.

There he is, still gawping at me, muzzle wide open. I can smell that he's scared out of his wits, and I can see the cogs in his mind turning. *Just keep your mouth shut, Frankie*, I think to myself. *Bide your time*. That always freaks humans out. Because then they start to wonder whether they're imagining things. 'Did that cat *really* just speak?' they ask themselves. 'Is this real? Or am I losing my mind?'

The man stares at me for quite a while. Then, when nothing happens, and I say nothing, he leans back in his armchair with a sigh of relief and shuts his muzzle again. He shakes his head and exclaims with a smile, 'What nonsense!'

'Oh no, it's not!' I reply.

This time, the man really loses it. His face goes as white as a deer's bum, which I must admit, I did enjoy a little. Well, more than a little if I'm being honest. It's always better when a human understands what you're capable of, or else you're never safe from them. They might even kick you or throw things at you. Now, at the very least, I had earned this man's respect.

A pause. Then in a flurry of confusion, the man yells, 'YOU CAN TALK?'

Congratulations, I think. *Top marks for observation.* He then proceeds to speak to me very loudly and very slowly. I once watched a film with Old Mrs Berkowitz where one group of men was sitting around a fire talking to another group of men with painted faces and a collection of feathers on their heads. They did exactly the same thing. I mean, the first ones spoke to the feathered ones as if they were total dimwits.

Tapping himself on the chest, the man says, 'ME. RICHARD. GOLD.'

This behaviour seemed pretty odd to me, but something about it was funny too. So I turn to the man and tap myself on the chest. 'ME. FRANKIE.'

'YOUR HEAD. HURT? OUCH?' he asks.

'YES. OUCH-OUCH!' I reply.

'ME. SORRY,' he says.

We fall silent, and the man doesn't seem to know what to say after that. Then he reaches out tentatively and lays his paw briefly on mine, saying 'YOU. NO. WORRY.'

That's a nice touch. And since he's being nice, I figure

there's no point beating around the bush. We might as well get down to business.

'MUNCHY-MUNCHY? HUNGER!' I tell him.

I point to my belly and my mouth.

Reassuring me, he replies, 'MUNCHY-MUNCHY? YOU? I FETCH FOOD!'

And if you ask me, those were the first sensible words the man named Richard Gold had spoken.

2. Frankie Boy

Just so you know: from now on, I'm going to call the man named Richard Gold 'Gold' for short. It's saves me time, which is just as well because this story's a bit on the longer side and we still have a way to go. Plus, I don't really like the name Richard. I know he can't help being called that. But let's face it, as names go, it's a bit of a non-starter.

And believe me, I've known some crap names in my time. My mother named me Number 5, and my siblings were called Number 1, Number 2, Number 3, Number 4, Number 6 and Number 8.

There wasn't a number 7, because my mother said it would bring bad luck. So Number 7 became Number 8, though he was officially the seventh sibling. Naturally, we nicknamed him 78 to add to the confusion.

Later, when I was living at the animal shelter, the humans there named me Milksop on account of my white chin. That all but ended any hopes I had of a respectable reputation. Oh the shame! The embarrassment!

All the other animals laughed at me. Even the miniature Pekinese in the next cage – who looked like a collage of animals that have long since gone extinct – joined in.

Eventually a family with children took me away and

gave me a new name: Herbert. Or sometimes Herr Bert. They thought it funny and – excuse me while I gag – *cute*.

But they were also cruel, and the children were the worst of all. They'd hold a lighter to my tail for a laugh, or would throw me back and forth to each other like a ball, shouting, 'Fly, Herr Bert!' One day, out of sheer terror, I clawed one of the children across their face. And then I did it again. It was a rather bloody affair. I wound up back at the shelter again after that.

And everyone knew me as Milksop once more.

But just when I started to think I'd be Milksop for the rest of my life, Old Mrs Berkowitz suddenly appeared in front of my cage. She looked at me, stroked my head and muttered, 'Milksop? Well, isn't that a shitty name!' She was quite the lady, but her language was often less than ladylike.

So now you know: if my lingo is sometimes a little on the coarse side, it's not my fault. Blame the educational deficiencies in my upbringing!

Then Old Mrs Berkowitz took me home with her and spent a few days thinking and listening to a lot of music. By a man from America who she called Frankie Boy Sinatra. Let me tell you, this Frankie Boy could really sing. Not a patch on a coal tit, mind. But he was pretty decent for a human. Anyway, Old Mrs Berkowitz says to me: 'Frankie. How do you like that name?' And I'm like: *Wow.* I was blown away. I went prancing through the village, calling out to everybody: 'I'm Frankie! As in Frankie Boy from America!'

So now you know how I got my marvellous name. But that's not what I meant to tell you.

I was going to say something completely different. But I'm easily distracted. That's why I keep telling myself: *you mustn't lose focus when you're telling a story, Frankie!* But it's not easy. Especially as I don't really know what a focus is. I sort of know. But not exactly. I know that it's something you mustn't lose. Anyway, where were we?

Ah yes. So, I'm lying on this couch in the Deserted House and I can hear the man who I'm going to call just Gold trudging around the house, opening and closing doors. As if he's hidden food everywhere. And the thought of food is driving me crazy. Other than grasshoppers and the end of an old sausage I found hanging out of a dustbin, I haven't a thing inside me. But I'm also scared stiff, of course. I don't know Gold. I don't know the Deserted House. At the same time, I'm super-curious, so I jump down off the couch and take a look around.

I'm still wobbly on my paws and immediately get the shock of my life: another tomcat! My tail goes as bushy as an old broom and I hiss at the intruder, until I realize there's something odd about him. He looks just like me. Only in black. And then the penny drops: I'm staring at the screen of a massive TV.

I've seen a few TV sets in my time, but this one is so vast it seems to go on for ever. Holy shit!

I'm a big fan of TV. Especially programmes with animals in them. My favourites are wildlife documentaries: the kind where penguins stand around for ages in a snowstorm, waiting by some hole in the ice for a fish to appear. I really don't get penguins, but I'd love to have a chat with one sometime. About their life.

Films with humans in them are boring. Whenever you see humans on TV, they're nearly always doing the same thing: beating up other humans. In every way imaginable. Why? I don't know. They don't even eat their kill!

The idea of lying here on the couch every night with my paw on the remote freaks me out. In a good way, I mean.

I carry on exploring the house, which is crammed full of books. There's no end to them; they're on shelves all over the place. If you ask me, books are rubbish. I looked inside one once, but all that was in it were lots of words, and it just made me yawn like mad. All the same, I've never seen such a nice house before. There are windows with wide windowsills, which is just the thing for a cat who likes to spend his time lounging, looking and sleeping. What strikes me as I'm wandering round having a good sniff is the *smell.* It doesn't smell like rotting mice or Fatty Heinz's pee, if that's what you're thinking. It smells . . . sort of sad, somehow. Like an old, abandoned fox den. I don't know if you've ever looked round any old, abandoned fox dens. But they don't have a good vibe either: everything smells of the past, and partings, and happy fox years that will never return.

It's the same in this place.

I go up some stairs, to find more rooms, and more books. But there's also a large bed, so I dive straight into it. It's a natural reflex. I start kneading away frantically on the soft bedspread, knead-knead-knead, until finally the purring kicks in. Another reflex.

I can't remember the last time I lay in a bed. But I can tell you where I live at the moment. On the way out of the village, right at the end of the Big Road, is a small mountain with a fence around it. This is where humans throw out everything they no longer want. Car tyres, chairs, radios, old socks – you name it. You wouldn't believe how much *stuff* humans need in their lives! They're mad about *stuff* and cram their houses full of it. And when their houses get too full, they throw some of the old stuff away and get new stuff. The Professor (who you'll meet later on) says this is a symptom of *civilization*. Humans are *civilized*, whereas we animals aren't. And to be civilized, you need a whole lot of stuff so you can impress other people and show everyone just how civilized you are. It's a bit like a horde of gorillas beating their chests and bigging themselves up. Anyway, I'm jolly glad humans are civilized enough to build me a nice mountain. I've never had any stuff in my whole life, apart from the little scarf around my neck. That was a present from Old Mrs Berkowitz, and I wear it in her memory.

But I was going to tell you where I live. Right at the top of the mountain, where all the human stuff is piled up, there's a rusty bathtub propped up against a big stone, with its legs sticking up in the air. And that bathtub – or rather the space under it – is where I live.

Living on a mountaintop has its advantages. There's the view, for a start, and the pure air. But it certainly has its downsides too. Like the raccoons who prowl around at night, scaring the shit out of you with their razor-sharp teeth.

In winter, I huddle right at the back of the bathtub on the icy ground, head on my paws, tail wrapped tight around me, scrawny tomcat arse shivering in the cold, with dreams of being in one of those houses with smoke billowing out of their chimneys, down in the village. So that's why I can't believe that I'm actually lying in this bed right now.

And then I start weighing up my options. OK, so Gold's an idiot. But not a very dangerous one, as far as I can judge. Plus, he has a guilty conscience. And he has that beautiful piece of string. *And* a ton of food. *And* the biggest TV in the world. *And* a super-soft bed. *And* all of this inside a house.

You're the clever ones: you do the maths!

Exactly . . . I've hit the jackpot!

Or so I thought. Until Gold came back inside.

'Hello?'

'Up here,' I say.

'Ah . . . I . . . FOOD . . . JARS . . .'

I can't understand a word and scoot downstairs. Gold is standing in the kitchen.

'I SEARCH. EVERYWHERE. BUT . . .'

Now I'm finally losing patience.

'Come on, that's enough now. Talk to me like a human being! What have you got to eat?'

Gold gawps at me and goes a bit white around the

chops again. Then he says: 'This is all I could find,' and plants two jars and a tin on the kitchen table.

The two jars and the tin are of no use to me at all. In the jars are some fat green fingers that Gold calls 'gherkins'. And in the tin are these yellow rings with a hole in the middle.

'Pineapple,' says Gold, offering me one of the yellow rings. 'It's . . . um . . . a sweet exotic fruit from the south. Latin America, for example. Or Africa. Pineapples grow on bushes, not trees.'

And straightaway I notice something. Gold has an odd way of talking. A little like a swan. Swans are always droning on about things that are of no interest to anyone. If I say to a swan on a lake: 'Hey, Swan! How's it hanging?', you can bet the swan will say: 'Well, I'm not actually hanging. I'm swimming. But thanks for asking, dear Mr Frankie! It's a good day for swimming, the water's mild, almost warm, although it's a bit choppy in the middle of the lake, a bit of a cold current from below, my wife always says . . .' And so on. And so forth. Rhubarb, rhubarb. That's why no one likes talking to swans. They're pompous types.

'Have you got any meat?' I ask.

Gold shakes his head.

'Or sausage? A piece of cheese, at least? I'm partial to Emmental.'

Gold shakes his head.

'What about quark? A drop of cream? No? Milk, perhaps?'

'I haven't got anything to eat! I'm sorry. If I had, I'd

give it to you. All of it. But I haven't been in the house for ages. Not since last year, when Linda . . . um . . . well, never mind. And I haven't done any shopping because . . . um, I mean: what for?' And he points at the string. To be honest, I didn't understand Gold's banter. But I understood that there was no grub. Just green fingers and rings with holes in them.

So I eat one of the rings with a hole in it, and it tastes sweet, very sweet, like the sweet spot behind a mouse's ear. Only much worse. So I pretend to myself that it's a mouse ear, and then I manage.

After I've finished, Gold opens the door and says: 'So, I guess you'll want to be off now. You must be impatient to get home. . .'

I take no notice. Instead, I slip past him into the lounge, jump back on the couch, stretch out and ask: 'Have you got cable? D'you like wildlife documentaries?'

Turns out he doesn't have cable, which is a shame.

'A giant TV and no cable?'

'Cancelled,' Gold says. He stands around in the kitchen for a moment, hesitating, then comes into the lounge with a bottle in his hand and sits down in the armchair opposite. And that's it.

Gold doesn't speak. Just sits staring at the string and pressing his forehead as if he's thinking. And I don't speak either, because I don't know what to say. Or do.

I had no idea how to conduct a real human conversation. Up until that point, I'd always just listened while humans did the talking. What's more, in my world you sniff each other first before you start chewing the fat. It's part of our culture. Say I meet a dog or another tomcat, for example, and he's not aggressive or totally mangy and lice-ridden, we have a good sniff. Tentatively at first. Then we stick our noses everywhere. And I mean *everywhere.*

It tells you an awful lot: age, place of residence, personality defects – that sort of thing. I did the same when I met my friend the Professor, who you'll meet later. We got right in there with our noses – front end, back end, the whole shebang. And when we came up for air, we knew: we're good to go!

It's different with humans though. At least, I've certainly never seen them sticking their noses in any part of each other's anatomy. And that's why it's so complicated getting into conversations with humans.

Gold still doesn't speak. Just carries on swigging from the bottle. He's drinking something that looks like water but doesn't smell like it. By now it's dark outside, and the whole room fills with silence. I can see this becoming a problem over time, in terms of the general *vibe.* Especially as we're living together now. I briefly consider jumping on to Gold's lap and offering him my bottom to sniff. As an ice-breaker, you know? But then suddenly, I end up speaking after all. The words just come tumbling out.

'D'you know Flipper?'

Gold looks at me as though I'd just crapped on the carpet.

'What?'

'Flipper! He's this super-smart dolphin who helps humans. On TV. One of my favourites. But I don't believe it.'

'What? What don't you believe?'

'I mean, I just don't believe a dolphin can be that clever. I know this carp, you see. In the lake here. Practically a dolphin, only smaller. And *he's* not very bright. Nothing upstairs. Have you ever met a smart carp? Or a dolphin?'

Once again, here I was, offering up some truly entertaining conversation. 'Unlike carp,' says Gold, 'dolphins aren't fish. Dolphins are mammals. Like whales.'

Then he goes silent again for ages. Carries on swigging from the bottle. He must have been mighty thirsty. And just as I'm thinking, *you're flogging a dead horse here, old chap*, Gold suddenly pipes up.

'Do you know Lassie?' he asks.

'You bet!' I reply.

'Lassie, oh my God! I always wanted a dog just like that as a kid. A collie! Beautiful, she was. I was crazy about Lassie.'

After that there's no stopping us. From Flipper and Lassie, we move on to Fury. Then Inspector Rex. And Kermit the Frog. King Kong, Bambi, Mister Ed, Garfield, penguins in general and the question of why Maya the Bee is such a bore.

'Are all bees smart-arses?' asks Gold.

'Most of them,' I say.

Gold knew lots of interesting things about animal celebrities. And lots of uninteresting things too. He talked about 'animals in literature' and asked whether I knew a Moby Dick, or a Miss-Toffee-Fleas, or some mentally challenged bear: Booh or Pooh, I think it was. The other problem was that Gold was getting harder and harder to understand. By now, the bottle was empty and he spoke as if he had a ball in his mouth. Eventually, Gold leans forward in his chair, with difficulty. His head is swaying and I can smell his bottle breath.

'Frankie, there's something I have to ask you. But be honest! Am I crazy? Be honest!'

I try to reassure him. 'Nah. I mean. I don't think so.'

'That just proves it! If you ask a cat if you're crazy and he answers you, then you must be crazy! That proves it!'

Then he goes quiet again, slumping miserably in his armchair. Finally, his eyes fall shut and he starts snoring like a pack of wolves. Still, it was a good conversation.

I creep upstairs to the room with the super-soft bed and slip inside. But I'm far too excited, so I jump on to the windowsill and look out at the moon, shining brightly over the little mountain with my old bathtub on top, and I think: *Frankie, you crazy cat. No one'll believe you when you tell 'em. Let's face it, you can't even believe it yourself.*

3. Consideration and Stuff

When day breaks, I start to feel restless. Gold is still slumped in his armchair downstairs asleep. I jump on to his lap: 'Hey, wake up!' Gold doesn't react. I poke him in the face with my paw, on the nose. Human noses are fun to poke because they're hairless and soft, a bit like a fat snail without a shell. Gold starts. Then he stares at me and says: 'Oh shit. You *are* real after all. It's not a dream.'

'I need a pee. Can you please . . .'

I point to the closed front door with my paw.

'What . . . what's the time?'

'No idea. I'm a cat. I don't have a watch.'

Gold looks at his tiny telephone, which lights up in the dark like a glow-worm.

'Half past four . . .'

'And?'

'That's early, very early.'

'I need a pee.'

'You'll have to hold it. No peeing before seven. Those are the house rules. My house, my rules.'

Gold closes his eyes.

I poke his nose again.

'Seven!' he says, and turns over.

I put my muzzle up close to his ear and speak into it directly like a mousehole. 'I. Need. A. Pee.'

'Go away!'

I let out a few yowls of desperation. But Gold doesn't budge. Then I jump down off the chair and start scratching the couch.

'Hey, what are you doing? Stop it!' Gold shouts.

'I am expressing my dissatisfaction with the whole situation.'

'By destroying my couch?'

'I need a pee.'

'And I need to sleep! It's the middle of the night and I'm not feeling very well. Not very well at all. Can't you show a bit of consideration? Thank you.'

'What's *consideration*?'

'Are you pulling my leg?'

'Which leg?'

'You know, are you having me on . . . taking the piss? Never mind. You want to know what consideration is?'

'No, I want a pee.'

'Jesus, you're a pain! Having consideration means respecting the needs of others.'

'Hmm. Sounds good. I need a pee!'

'Others' needs! Not your own.'

'OK.'

'Really?'

'Nah.'

'Look: I'm going to show consideration to you now by getting up and opening the door. Then, when you come back in, you will show me consideration by keeping your trap shut and letting me sleep.'

'Fine,' I say. 'That's a deal.'

*

But it wasn't fine of course. As I'm peeing in an overgrown flowerbed, listening out for animal noises and looking up at the sky, I think to myself: *Consideration? Lunacy more like!* If a hungry eagle starts circling above me now, he's hardly going to say: 'I'm coming for you! But do finish what you're doing first, Frankie. I'm nothing if not *considerate*.'

To which I would reply, 'Gee, thanks, Eagle.'

And he'd reply: 'Don't mention it, Frankie. Considering others is everything.'

Humans often have no idea. But if you live with a human, one thing is essential: you have to set boundaries! And show them who's boss. Otherwise they'll walk all over you and want to call all the shots. They'll impose rules on you by using words like *consideration*. And before you know it, you can't do anything without their permission: you can only pee when they say you can, only sleep where they say you can. Or, worst of all, you could end up like Fatty Heinz – and all thanks to a bit of consideration!

Fatty Heinz lives round the corner from the Deserted House, on the Big Road. He's not exactly the brightest spark in the pack, though he can't help that of course. And sometimes I feel sorry for him, having to run around every day after a piece of tree his human throws across the massive garden. It's always the same: the human sits on a bench by the house, stretching out his short little legs and smoking. The human is called Mr Kaufmann and is also fat. Even fatter than Fatty Heinz.

Just so you can picture the scene, when Mr Kaufmann throws the piece of tree, his whole body wobbles. Then Fatty Heinz shoots off after the piece of wood and drops it at Mr Kaufmann's feet. And the whole thing starts all over again.

Throwing.

Running.

Throwing.

Running.

And so it goes on.

Before long, half the village can hear Fatty Heinz wheezing, and everyone wonders if he's about to breathe his last. All except Mr Kaufmann, who cries: 'Yes, you like that, my boy, don't you?'

Once, I asked Fatty Heinz whether he does like it.

'Heinz, why do you do that thing with the piece of tree? It's a fool's game. You're running around like an idiot.'

'I know, mate. But I've no choice,' he replied.

'No?'

'Nah.'

'D'you wanna talk about it?'

'I do it for my human. Because I think he likes it. And my human does it for me. Because he thinks I like it.'

'I see. A vicious cycle.'

'Exactly.'

I imagine dogs all over the world running after some old piece of tree just because they can't bring themselves to tell their humans the truth. Or as smart-arse

Gold would say: because they're being considerate. And that's why consideration gets you nowhere, if you ask me, especially if you're an animal.

I slip back into the house. Gold has moved and is now asleep on the couch, wrapped in a blanket. I poke him on the nose with my paw, crying: 'Hey, wake up! I'm hungry!'

And because I'm being considerate, I only poke him three times.

But the problem is that there's no food. And a second problem is that Gold isn't the slightest bit interested in the first problem. All he does is lie there. First, he sleeps on the couch, then he sits staring into the distance. And this is strange because, as far as I know, humans are always doing something. Working, usually. They sweat and toil until they've chopped down a forest or built a house or shovelled three piles of sand from left to right or drilled a hole in something. For anyone who isn't a human, this constant labouring can really get on your nerves because it causes trouble and disturbs the peace. But in this case, I would have been glad if Gold *had* done something. To see him lying there not lifting a finger was just odd.

'I'm hungry!' I yowl again. But this time I give looking extra cute a try: this strategy never fails with humans. This is how to *look cute*: you tilt your head to one side, pout, bend your ears down slightly, open your eyes wide and – most importantly – pour everything you can into that look. Love, anticipation, pain, longing, and so on. But you need to get the balance right, mind. Too much pain is no good, because then your human won't think: *Aah, how cute!* They'll think, *Uh-oh, bowel problems.*

But even the cute number falls flat with Gold.

'Go and catch a mouse,' he says, waving me away.

Now I'm getting really uneasy. Something's not right.

'Aren't you hungry?' I ask. 'Surely you must want to eat too?'

'I've gone off eating,' Gold says. 'It doesn't matter. Nothing matters.'

That was even weirder than the lying around and staring into space business. I know all sorts of people, and some of them are pretty peculiar, I can tell you: owls, swans, dogs, a one-eyed badger, a magpie with hiccups and a sheep called Attila the Hun. But I don't know anyone who would say they'd gone off eating and that *nothing mattered* to them. I bet even a dung beetle who does nothing but roll dung all day long wouldn't go that far. To him, a pile of crap is always interesting.

I jump on to the windowsill, look out at the garden despondently and start to think. If nothing matters to Gold any more, then logic tells me I don't matter to him either. So my grand plan to live in the Deserted House and hit the jackpot and so on is out the window. This is a problem.

But then suddenly, something happens. As things often do in stories, and in life.

Through the window, I see a small white car driving up the Big Road. It stops right outside the Deserted

House and a woman gets out. A woman with a briefcase. She rings the gate buzzer.

'A visitor,' I say.

'Shit,' says Gold.

4. Little Pooshock

The woman with the briefcase rings twice more and when no one answers, she opens the gate, crosses the garden and walks up to the house. Gold, who has been watching all this, jumps up from the couch and moves towards the door. Then he comes running back, climbs on a chair and hastily takes down the string that's still dangling from the ceiling. He hesitates for a moment, wondering what to do with it, then chucks it behind the couch and dashes back to the front door. I creep along cautiously in his wake, then hide in the kitchen and peer round the corner.

Gold has opened the front door and is talking to the woman. She sounds young. Younger than Gold, at any rate. But don't ask me what she looked like. No idea! And I can't tell you exactly what Gold looks like either, in case you've been wondering all this time.

Sorry about that. I'm told that when humans write books, they usually go into great descriptive detail about the human characters in them. Or they might describe a tree. Or the colour of the sky. That's what the people at the publishers told me. Apparently the humans who read the books want to have a picture in their head. The publishing people read me an example from a book by this famous writer, What's-his-name, who goes on endlessly about a human scratching his foot and drinking from a rusty tap and then scratching his foot again. Most impressive.

But I'm a cat, and to me, all humans look the same. They have an oval-shaped middle part, four long legs with a paw on each end, and a massive head. And that's it. No one even thought to give them any fur, other than a few tufts in places that make no sense. Whoever made humans didn't make much of an effort, if you ask me.

And now I'm finally getting to the point: the way I tell humans apart is by their smell and the sound of their voice. The woman with the briefcase smelt of flowers and grass and milk. Gold smelt of dust and wet leaves and the water from the bottle that wasn't water. Gold's voice hummed and thrummed like a swarm of bumblebees. The woman's made more of a cheeping noise. Like a house sparrow, but brighter and harsher, like a field sparrow. I hear the cheepy voice say to Gold: 'You phoned us. About a dead cat.'

'Oh . . . yes!' says Gold. 'The vets. And you are?'

'Anna Komarova, veterinary surgeon. Is the animal here in the garden?'

'No. I mean . . . not any more. I think it's all sorted now, anyway.'

'Sorted?'

'I made a mistake. The . . . the cat is alive. I'm sorry, I should have let you know.'

'So first the cat was dead, and now he's resurrected? Like Jesus?' says the woman called Anna Komarova, laughing.

'Listen, I'm really sorry for the wasted journey . . .' Gold sounds irritated. Super-irritated.

'Any sign of the cat?'

'Sign?'

'Did you see him again? Perhaps he was injured and is lying in the bushes here somewhere.'

Anna Komarova glances around the garden.

'No, no. There's nothing there. You can go now, don't worry. Believe me, that tomcat's fine.'

'Are you sure? And how do you know it's a tomcat? Did you examine the animal?'

'What? No! Of course not. He told me . . . I mean, *he* didn't tell me, obviously. I told myself. Must be a tomcat, I said to myself, when I saw him lying there. Simple as that.'

Anna Komarova looks at Gold as if he's two sandwiches short of a picnic. 'Let me get this straight: first there was a, shall we say, cat-like animal lying here in the garden. Then you looked at it and said to yourself: ah, that must be a tomcat. And it's dead. So you rang us at the practice. Then the dead tomcat was no longer dead, but . . . gone. And so now you believe that he's alive. But you haven't seen him since. And even though you haven't seen him since, you are quite certain that he isn't injured. Which is why you haven't even had a quick scout around your garden, as any normal person would do having just found a cat there. Especially a dead one who then has suddenly disappeared. Do you realize how that sounds to me?'

Gold nods. 'OK.' He pauses. 'OK,' he says again,

looking at Anna Komarova as if he is about to bite her head off. But she returns the look. It was like two rutting stags, I tell you, squaring up to each other at dawn, ready to lock antlers.

'You don't give up, do you?' Gold says.

'Not when the story's quite so ludicrous, no.'

'OK. Fine. If you insist. The cat's in the house. You're welcome to take him. I don't care. In fact, you'll be doing me a favour. Frankie! There's a visitor here for you.'

And that's how I met Anna Komarova. She squats down in front of me, smiles and says: 'Hello, Frankie. I'm Anna.'

She doesn't touch me straightaway, but holds out her paw first for me to sniff, which personally I found to be quite polite and a rather nice gesture.

'I'm going to examine you first, OK?' she says. 'Don't be scared. It won't take long and it won't hurt.'

Both of these things were lies.

This Anna Komarova speaks a funny sort of Humanish. I mean, it sounds funny. 'Pooshock, ah, my little Pooshock,' she says to me, and hums away to herself as she rummages in her briefcase. *Poo socks?* I think, indignantly. *How dare you?* Then, as if she could read my mind, she says:

'Pooshock is a common name for a tomcat in Russia. My little Pooshock.'

And that's another thing I'll never understand: why are there so many different types of Humanish? I once met a tomcat at the shelter called Juan who came from somewhere in Far-Away-Land. A place called *Spain* or something like that. But it wasn't a problem. Because Juan didn't speak Spain-Cattish, if that's what you were thinking. He just spoke ordinary Cattish, like the rest of us. That's the only kind of Cattish there is. And everyone sticks to it. At least, I do.

'Hey, Juan, what's it like in Spain?'

'Warm,' Juan replies.

'And the mollies?'

'They're hot, amigo,' he nods.

We ended up having a really good conversation, and I learnt a whole lot about Spain. Apparently the people there eat dried bull and fight with squid in an arena and do all kinds of other weird stuff. But just imagine if it were two humans talking, one from Far-Away-Land and the other from Up-the-Road. Hopeless! Neither would understand the other, they'd just sit scratching their heads all day thinking: *Huh?* And that has to be the dumbest thing in the world.

I'd rather not tell you what happened next. But I will. Anna Komarova says: 'Now be brave, my little Pooshock,' and starts kneading my head. First around my left ear, which has a whole chunk missing where a raccoon once bit me with its razor-sharp teeth. Raccoons are scumbags who steal other animals' ears.

Next, Anna Komarova kneads around the sore place where the Thing pounced on me. 'Dear, oh dear, my poor little Pooshock,' she says, as she squeezes a few drops of something on to it. The stuff burns like hell and makes me yowl so pitifully it's embarrassing. Then suddenly this arrow pricks me, so now I'm yowling *and* hissing. And while I'm busy yowling and hissing, Anna Komarova sticks something up my rear. A small, cold stick. I'm being attacked on all sides! Before I can think about what's going on in my back end, Anna Komarova is already at my front end again. She prises my muzzle open and shoves something inside. 'Dewormer,' she says.

I feel like the grubbiest tomcat under the sun. Then Anna Komarova turns me upside down, pulls my paws apart and pokes around in my fur.

'Ah, good, you're castrated, my little Pooshock,' she says. Then she lets me go and I scoot under the couch where I crouch, arse to the wall, quaking with fear and anger. Humans! Why do you do this? Molesting a fine specimen of a tomcat like me and pricking him with arrows, smearing burning stuff on his head. Is this your idea of fun? Are you honestly so cruel? And why am I *castrated*?

To be honest, I don't know what *castrated* means. But surely I'd know – or at least feel – if I was. And someone would surely have said to me by now: 'Hey, Frankie, you look a bit castrated today.' But that's humans for you. Always spouting daft ideas about animals and throwing fancy words around because they think they're the only ones who can understand them. That way they can feel superior, like they rule the world.

While I'm trembling there under the couch, Gold and Anna Komarova are having a conversation. I might not have caught all of it. Because I'm still in shock, and besides, you can't hear very well under a couch anyway. But this much I can make out:

'Here are some tablets,' Anna Komarova says. 'Give him one daily. For five days. To stop the wound on his head from getting infected.'

'I can't look after him,' says Gold. 'I'm . . . I have to go away. He's not my cat. Please take him with you.'

'We're vets, we're not an animal shelter.'

'I really can't do it, I'm sorry.'

'What's your problem?'

'*I'm* the problem,' says Gold.

'Cat allergy?'

'What? No . . .'

'Well then. Looking after an animal for five days, pampering it a bit: even a child can do that. Don't be an arsehole. And buy him something decent to eat. He's much too thin. Here's the address of the pet shop. You can get everything there. I'll pop round again and check up on him. Be good to him, my little Pooshock.'

And with that, Anna Komarova leaves. She gets into her small car and screeches off up the Big Road.

Five days, I think.

5. Hail the Supreme Commander

I nod off for a moment before waking up again. Eventually, Gold comes over and stands in front of the couch.

'Frankie, are you still down there?'

'I might be,' I whisper.

'I'm going out,' Gold says.

'Out? Where to?'

'Errands, shopping,' says Gold.

'To the Pet Shop?'

'Yes, maybe.'

I creep out from under the couch.

'I'm coming with you.'

'No way. I'll be back soon.'

'I'm coming with you.'

'In this house the SCC applies, Frankie.'

'SCC?'

'Standard Code of Conduct. In other words, you do as I say. And rule number one is: don't rile me up. Otherwise I won't be very pleasant company.'

'Are you riled up right now?'

'Not particularly at the moment. But that could change.'

'Ah, I see. Very interesting.'

And then I simply follow Gold out to the car, whether he likes it or not, and when he opens the door, I scoot past him on to the passenger seat. Piece of cake. After a quick sniff round, I settle down next to Gold. 'Ready when you are,' I say. For a second he glares at me, as if he's about to grab me and throw me out, but then with an 'Oh, sod it' he puts his foot to the pedal.

Now, you're probably thinking: *what's a tomcat doing going shopping? That's crazy!* But I didn't trust Gold. 'I can't look after him,' he had said to Anna Komarova. So I reckoned he was probably planning to just up and leave. Without me. Because that's what humans are like. I've seen it myself. No sooner had Old Mrs Berkowitz fetched me from the shelter than she was gone. From one day to the next. Driven away in the white car with the lights on the roof. Without so much as a goodbye. And that's how I ended up here.

What's more, my ears pricked up at hearing the words *Pet Shop*. I once knew a fox who knew a terrier who had an uncle who once went to the Pet Shop. Or so the fox told me. Anyway, according to him the Pet Shop is a place where the humans serve the animals. In white overalls and super-polite and in all animal languages and everything. They even greet you with food at the entrance and ask you: 'What would you like to eat? Dry or wet? Regional or international?' If you have luggage with you, say you're a packhorse or something, then a human will come rushing up and carry it for you. But you can also have humans stroke, delouse, massage or groom you. Or you can bathe in catnip, or spend all day watching wildlife documentaries about penguins.

So obviously I reply with a 'Wow, Fox! That sounds awesome!'

And he's like: 'Pet Shops are the best place on earth. Take it from me.'

Mind you, foxes do tell a lot of porkies. Or rather, they're always exaggerating. It's in their nature. It doesn't bother me, because they don't mean any harm. If you meet a fox in the woods and ask: 'Is it far to the river?', then you can bet the fox will say: 'Just round the corner, my friend!' when it's half a day's slog. But I'll say this for foxes: they never have a bad word to say about anything or anyone. Always positive. Always sunshine and roses. That's why they get invited to speak at funerals so often. No one invites them to chicken funerals though, obviously. At all the funerals I've ever been to, a fox has always read the eulogy. You can count on everyone crying hysterically by the end, and saying much nicer things about the dead person than when they were alive. So if the Pet Shop was half as good as the fox made out, then I definitely wanted to go there.

We drive slowly along the Big Road through the village. Whenever I see anyone, human or animal, I wave a paw at them. Like I'm royalty, or a president. I've seen kings and presidents on TV, and that's what they do every day: drive around and wave. Why, I don't know. But if I had to work all day, like humans are always doing, that's the job I'd choose. At any rate, I'd make a good president if you're ever in need of one.

Once we're out of the village, we speed up and I gaze out of the window: everywhere you look there's new scenery, places I've never been, foreign territories. Incredible, isn't it? Just how big the world is? So many sights and smells and sounds to explore!

The trouble is, though, I'm being shaken all over the place and there's a constant roaring in my ears. Trees, bushes and even clouds are flashing past me. It's making me quite ill. When did trees start whizzing around like that? First, I start yawning, then switch to miaowing miserably, feeling wretched and forlorn. I'm so nauseous. Why on earth did I get into this car? *Frankie, you're an idiot*, I think to myself.

'What's up?' asks Gold.

'I don't feel well.' He slows down.

'Thanks.' I yawn, lying flat on my tummy.

'Don't you dare throw up all over the car,' says Gold. 'I'll have you know you're in an 86 Benz 280 SL.'

'Sure,' I say. No idea what he's on about. There isn't much space in the car and it has an odd smell, a bit like wet dog. And it only has two seats. I'm guessing it's a car for poor people.

Gold presses a button and the window glides down. A blast of air flows in. He puts some music on, a faint tinkling and tooting.

'Concentrate on the music and breathe,' says Gold. 'Linda often felt sick in the car. You need to breathe consciously in and out. That helps.'

'Who's Linda?' I ask, breathing deeply.

'My wife.'

Damn, I think. You never know where you stand with humans; one's enough trouble as it is. But two?

'You have a wife?'

'Had,' says Gold. 'Not any more.'

Phew, lucky escape, I think.

'And where is she now? New turf?'

'You could say that. In heaven,' says Gold, pointing upwards.

'In the sky? With the birds, you mean?'

The idea of a human flying around up there strikes me as highly unlikely.

'With God. If there is a God.'

'Heaven? God? I don't understand . . .'

'You're supposed to breathe, not chatter!'

'I can breathe *and* chat. Who's God?'

'You're not religious?'

'Is religious the same thing as castrated?'

'Not exactly. God is, well, He's the boss. He created the world. God guides and protects people. If you're religious, it means you believe in God.'

'Ah, the Supreme Commander!'

'Exactly. You believe in a *Supreme Commander*?'

'Some dogs do. Especially the aggressive sort – the ones who aren't all that bright. Pitbulls, Dobermans, bull dogs and the like. They think there's a Supreme Commander. The Supreme Commander used to be called Blondie before he became the Supreme Commander.'

'Blondie?'

'So I've heard. He's supposed to be really ancient, and a German shepherd. But a giant one. With a giant muzzle and giant teeth, and he lives somewhere high up on a giant mountain, in a giant kennel, and sometimes he barks wise instructions down from the mountaintop, and everyone must follow them. Though who knows, maybe they're not so wise.'

'What do you think?'

'I don't know whether the Supreme Commander exists or not.'

'So you're agnostic?'

'Sure.'

'Do you know what an agnostic is?'

'Someone who sells glasses.'

'That's an optician.'

'Whatever. So agnostics don't sell glasses?'

'I'm sure some opticians are agnostics too.'

'There you go then.'

'But that's not the same thing!'

'I didn't say it was! Ooh, I feel sick. Boy, do I feel sick!'

The road's getting bumpier now, and the car suddenly starts bouncing up and down, up and down, as if we're surfing. Not that I've ever been surfing. But you know what I mean. Gold puts his hand on my head, though alas, only briefly, as if he's afraid to. His hand is big and heavy, and my head almost disappears into it like in a cave. It's a reassuring feeling. I close my eyes and breathe – consciously in, consciously out – and listen to the tinkly music. But talking is the best distraction.

'Why was your wife so keen to go to heaven? It's a hell of a long way away.'

'My wife's dead,' says Gold.

And that's when the penny finally drops, though I still have some unanswered questions.

'Heaven isn't an actual place,' says Gold. 'It's more of a . . . metaphor. A comforting thought, you see?'

'Not really.'

'A lot of people believe in life after death. The dead person's soul goes up to heaven. And then it's with God. Heaven is where God is.'

'Do I have a *soul* too?'

'Yes. All living things do.'

'Cool. What's a soul?'

'D'you really want to know? The soul is – how shall I put it? – the immortal part of you. Your feelings, thoughts, experiences. The quintessence of your being.'

All this stuff seems very complicated to me. Metaphors, quintessence and suchlike. Still, it sounds like it's still good to have a soul though, just in case. After all, you never know what's round the corner, and when you might need one. Besides, I'm an agnostic now. I'm guessing all agnostics must have a soul, otherwise they couldn't be agnostics. But I don't know for sure.

'Are you an agnostic too?' I ask.

'I'm an atheist,' says Gold. 'At least, that's what I always thought.'

I think it better not to ask what an atheist is. My head might explode. And Gold doesn't explain either. You'll have to find that out for yourselves, I'm afraid.

I turn over on to my back, paws in the air: my favourite position for dozing. But I can't doze. My stomach is all over the place. I look out of the window at the sky, which is very blue – even bluer than a forget-me-not – and mind-blowingly huge. It just goes on and on. We've been driving for quite a while by now (further than I've ever been in my life) and the sky is still there. It's coming as a real shock to learn that you can't seem to run away from the sky. Particularly now that I'm imagining masses of humans flying around up there in heaven, together with God and a whole bunch of souls and atheists and opticians and Gold's wife. Perhaps even Old Mrs Berkowitz too. It does my head in just thinking about it. Especially if you factor in birds and aeroplanes as well. It must be chaos up there! But there's something wonderful about it all the same.

Eerie and wonderful. And then I think about how I might live in heaven too one day, or my soul would, if agnostics really do have a soul. In all honesty though, I didn't really fancy the idea. The journey to the Pet Shop was bad enough. I'd never make it all the way to heaven. That was one thing I was sure of.

6. Cat on a Leash

We stop in front of a flat building like a giant yellow box planted in the landscape.

'That's the Pet Shop?'

'Looks like it,' says Gold.

There are other, similar boxes, lots of them, and humans are hurrying in and out of the boxes, carrying bags which they load into their cars before driving away, to be instantly replaced by new cars with new humans, who emerge from the boxes in their turn carrying more bags. And so it goes, on and on. Like ants, I think to myself.

We get out and I have a quick stretch, though with ears pricked. It's all so terribly noisy and strange here.

'Ready?' asks Gold.

'Born ready,' I say.

'OK. Once we're inside, you're not to talk. Got it?'

'Why not?'

'You can start not talking right about now.'

'But perhaps I have things to say.'

'Do you know what this is? Look carefully!'

Gold makes a curious sign by spreading two fingers of his right paw.

'How should I know what it is?'

'It's the silent fox. When you see the silent fox, keep your trap shut and don't annoy me!'

'There's no such thing as a silent fox. I'd know if there was. There's a red fox. And an Arctic fox. And a Twentieth-Century Fox, and a . . .'

'Frankie! Silent fox!'

And then Gold goes up to the entrance of the Pet Shop. I keep a short distance behind him in case we're attacked. And anyway, there's a door there, and doors are a problem. Doors get in a cat's way and won't move aside, even when you ask them nicely. But then the door opens all by itself, and I nearly die of shock. There's absolutely no one opening and closing the door, or if there is, they're either very well hidden or invisible. But I don't think so. At any rate, it's a moment of great wonder for me. A truly magical door.

Before I know it, I'm inside the Pet Shop. Though no one comes to serve me. No one is wearing white overalls. And no one is speaking any animal languages. That damned fox!

Instead, a very large woman comes rushing up to us, waving her arms around like an idiot and shouting: 'Hey! That's not allowed! Hey!' I hide behind Gold's legs.

'What do you think you're doing?' she says, pointing to me as she stands panting in front of us. The large woman is dressed from head to toe in yellow, like a giant Brimstone butterfly. Presumably one of the Pet Shop humans who work here.

'What's all this?' asks Gold.

'Is that your cat?'

'Tomcat,' says Gold. 'He's quite sensitive about that.'

'You can't bring pets in here.'

'Can't I?'

'Now don't you get funny with me, sir!'

'But this is a Pet Shop, isn't it?'

'Yes, of course we're a Pet Shop! But that doesn't mean you can bring pets in willy-nilly. You'll have to leave the cat outside.'

'Tomcat,' says Gold.

At that moment a woman walks through the magic door with a dog, a red setter, on a leash. In case you've never met a setter: to say they're incredibly vain is an understatement. Setters think of themselves as having the sleekest coats and cutest muzzles, and they think the rest of them is *super-cute* and *super-sleek* too. All I'm saying is that setters hold their noses so high in the air they can't even smell their own farts.

Anyway, this setter says to me, 'Hey, Tom. How's it going?'

'Hey, Setter. You're looking good,' I reply.

'I know. Even more than usual today, don't you think?'

I nod, adding, 'Bit of a situation with the Brimstone here.'

Setter: 'Sorry to hear it, mate. Good luck with that! I'll be at the back, in the Coat & Paw Care department.'

And they saunter on past, the woman and the setter, as if they had every right to be there.

'Why is the dog allowed in?' asks Gold.

'Dogs can come in, on the leash. Those are *the rules.* It's all written up on the door,' says Brimstone.

'But that's . . . racist,' says Gold.

'What? What are you talking about?' says Brimstone.

'Dogs are OK, but cats aren't? You're favouring one animal over another. You're discriminating based on species.'

'I never discriminate against anyone!'

'You know what? I'm going to put all this down in writing sometime. I'm a journalist, you see. Oh, that'll make a great headline: "Racist Regime at Pet Shop". And I'll make you the main feature and call you the Vertically Challenged Yellow Racist Pig from the Pet Shop.'

'Now look here, that's enough! You're off your rocker, you are! And I'm not a racist pig!'

All this time I'm looking on, thinking: *Racist?* And suddenly I stumble on an idea: why not collect all these complicated human words that are constantly whizzing about my ears and have a stab at explaining them to other animals? There's a big fat book for humans called *Brehm's Life of Animals*. Old Mrs Berkowitz was always consulting it. It's full of stuff about animals. But is there a big fat book for animals that's full of stuff about humans? Exactly!

From *Frankie's Life of Humans*:

> Racist (n.):
> *Large yellow woman resembling a Brimstone butterfly. Works at the Pet Shop. Says yes to dogs, no to cats.*
>
> Racist Pig (n.):
> *Not a pig at all, but a large yellow woman resembling a Brimstone butterfly. Works at the Pet Shop. Says yes to dogs, no to cats.*

The trouble is, my friends, I fear I'm too lazy to write such a big, fat book. Sometimes you have to be realistic about these things.

Gold and the Brimstone carry on arguing, and I can't think why Gold's getting so worked up about it all. He keeps repeating the words 'racist' and 'Nazi pig', until the Brimstone wells up with tears, and I suddenly feel sorry for her. It's like toying with a frightened, half-dead mouse just for the hell of it, and . . . Hang on a second . . . Bad example. Forget the mouse.

'OK, then put the cat on a leash,' Brimstone finally says.

'Tomcat,' says Gold. 'If you insist. Can you lend me a leash?'

Brimstone stomps off, presumably to fetch a leash, and I turn to Gold.

'No way am I going on a leash!'

'Oh, come on, Frankie.'

'Never!'

'Just this once. No one will know.'

'*I'll* know!'

'Look at the setter – he's on a leash.'

'But he's a *dog*!'

'Yes, so I see.'

'No, you don't see! Look, there are five types of animal: stable animals, herd animals, pack animals, leash animals and free animals. Plus a few subspecies and hybrids. Free animals – *like me* – are highly respected. They come right at the top. Pack animals, herd animals and stable animals are, well, let's say mid-level. But leash animals are right at the bottom, because they willingly let humans make slaves of them. *Leash animal* – now, that's a real insult! A thrush once called me a leash animal. I bit her head off on the spot.'

'OK, OK. I get the problem. No leash. Wait outside then.'

'But I want to come in. I'm a pet and I have a right to shop at the Pet Shop!'

'Have you got any money?'

'What? Of course not.'

'Well then. No leash. No money. It's not looking good for you.' At this point, Brimstone returns with a leash in her hand and looks at me with a grin on her face. Gold looks at me too. And there I am, so close to paradise, thinking: *Shit, Frankie.*

I'd appreciate it if you'd keep this story to yourself, OK? Embarrassing doesn't cover it. As we make our way through the Pet Shop, I'm praying no one will see me like this, on the end of a leash. Gold thinks the whole thing is hilarious. He's saying things like: 'Heel, Frankie!' and 'Sit, Frankie!' A man with a very simple sense of humour.

But back to the Pet Shop. The place is crammed full of stuff. I've never seen anything like it, my friends! Cushions, beds, bowls, combs, toothbrushes, paw cream, sweaters, shoes, among other things. I must say I don't know any animal that wears a sweater, not even slugs, and they could really do with one, on account of them not having a shell and all that. But I'm quite touched by the idea of humans making sweaters specially for them. It seems there are some humans who spend their days doing nothing but inventing stuff for animals. You can just imagine them at the pet shop factory, sitting there day after day with their sausage sandwiches, brooding over feeding bowls or dog whistles.

Human 1 might say: Hey, folks, can we have your attention for a moment? Our colleague has something to show you.

Human 2 would reply: I've given this some thought, and here's what I've come up with: a shoe for frogs! Because frogs, right, they do a lot of hopping about in ponds with nothing on their feet. What's more, this shoe's waterproof.

Human 1: Good work, mate!

Human 3: Not being funny or anything, but aren't frogs' feet already waterproof?

Human 2: Are you sure?

Human 3: Pretty sure, yes.

Human 2: OK, my mistake. What about this then: a toilet for beavers? Made of wood. Easy home assembly.

And everyone's like: Wow, that's so practical, mate! Those beavers will be super-grateful!

And they all clap until their hands are quite red.

I'm feeling quite happy, lost in this daydream. But after moseying around the Pet Shop for a while, I notice something's not quite right. In among all the pet supplies are cages. And sitting in one of them is a green parakeet. On a wooden swing. He sits staring straight ahead, then suddenly pecks at his feathers, plucks one out and jerks his head from side to side. Then he does the same again.

Staring.

Pecking.

Jerking.

Staring.

Pecking.

So I shout up to him, 'Hey, Parakeet, everything OK?'

But he doesn't say a word.

To be honest, I don't have much time for birds. Some of them are good singers, and once when I was lovesick and lay next to my old bathtub gazing up at the stars, a nightingale sang and I could have miaowed all night because it was so beautiful and my heart was aching so. But most birds just crap on your head. I once knew a cuckoo who used to fly away in the autumn and come back again in the spring.

'Hey Frankie, guess where I've just come from?' the Cuckoo would ask.

'Who cares? Don't crap on my head!' I'd reply.

'Africa! Have you ever been to Africa?'

'Nah.'

'Ah so you're a provincial, eh?'

'Provincial?'

'A country bumpkin! Guess you don't get out much?'

'Well, this is my patch.'

'I'm an incredible polyglot, you know. Can't help it. It's a lifestyle. Incredibly exciting, eh?'

'Polyglot *my arse.*'

'Oh, Frankie. I wish you could see all the things I see. Africa. The ocean. Lions. Penguins . . .'

'Penguins! No kidding?'

'Of course, silly. But I've just remembered: you can't go to Africa. No wings! Oh, you poor, poor chap.'

'Ah, buzz off, will you!'

And eventually he did. At least, so I thought. Till I felt something wet splat on my head.

That's migratory birds for you.

But with the parakeet in the cage, it was a very different story. A picture of misery. There's that swing for a start: what do you humans think a parakeet does all day in the wild? Sit on a swing in the forest? And if you're so delighted by this parakeet, why lock him up? Is this your way of showing affection?

'Open the cage,' I say to Gold.

'We'll get into trouble, Frankie.'

'Go on, open it!'

Gold looks around for the Brimstone. Then he quickly opens the cage door. 'Go on, get out of here, Parakeet!' I shout. 'Fly!' But the parakeet doesn't budge. Like he's nailed down. He carries on staring, pecking his plumage like mad, plucking one feather out after another. I'd never seen anything sadder. A parakeet who had forgotten how to be a parakeet.

We move on, past more and more stuff: transparent

boxes with fish living inside them and fake mice that squeak in fake Mousish when you squish their tummies – until we reach the cat section.

'What do you want to eat?' asks Gold, rummaging around on a huge shelf.

No one has ever asked me that before. What would I like to eat? When you live under an old bathtub on a rubbish heap, you're lucky to get *anything* to eat. I've chewed on some things in my time, I can tell you! There was this run-over hedgehog on the road once, lying there baking in the sun. Half of it was totally flattened. The other half was still a hedgehog, with a face and everything. But I was hungry, so I sat by the roadside chewing on this dried hedgehog nose – the only bit without prickles – thinking: *could be worse*. Flavour-wise, I mean. But not by much though.

'There's trout, turkey, venison, Alpine beef . . .'

'Beef?' I ask.

'Have a look.'

Gold lifts me up and sits me on his shoulder. And sure enough: beef. And prawn, and kangaroo, and tuna, even reindeer, though I don't even know what a reindeer looks like. And it's all in these shiny packets with a picture of a bored cat on the front, nibbling daintily from the plate as if it were a human with fur. 'Delicious reindeer with chicken, served with tasty baby carrots,' Gold reads to me.

I have eaten cat food before, of course. Plenty of the stuff. But I never knew what was in it. It was just the mush that Old Mrs Berkowitz used to put down in front of me. I liked it then. But I'm starting to find this all a little strange. Why beef? How's that supposed to work? I've never heard of a cat eating a cow, not in real life at least. Or a deer, for that matter. Or sailing around in a boat fishing for prawns or giant tuna. Yet suddenly, here it is, in the cat food. Could it be that you humans want cats who behave more like you do? Gold puts some cat food in the trolley (I tell him anything but reindeer, because he says reindeer come from Sweden, and that it's terribly cold there, and I prefer to eat my animals warm), and then we make our way back towards the magic door. We pass things called *cat trees*, which don't look anything like trees. We pass miniature houses which aren't houses at all but *cat toilets*. Out of curiosity I peer inside one of them, sit down and sniff around; it's dark and cramped like a rabbit burrow. Cat toilets are pretty pointless if you ask me. After all, the whole world is a toilet. I know humans have toilets though. Wherever a human installs himself, he installs a toilet. The two things go together. They're inseparable. And then it suddenly strikes me that if I had a toilet and it was installed at Gold's house, then I would be installed there too. And not just for five days, but for ever. Having your own toilet is the human's way of marking out his territory. Do you see?

'I want a toilet,' I say, and sit down.

'Why?' asks Gold.

'Hygiene,' I say.

'And who's going to clean this toilet?'

I look at Gold: 'Well, I can hardly do it myself,' I say, holding out my paws.

Surprisingly, Gold makes no further protest. He just nods mutely, like someone who couldn't care less. Then he picks up the toilet and a bag of cat litter, and soon we're back at the checkout with the Brimstone. She takes the leash off me and we exit through the magic door. I'm glad to be out of there, because the Pet Shop is clearly no place for pets. Only for humans with pets. And that's something else entirely.

Just then, I hear a whirring sound. It gets closer and closer and, turning around, I see the green parakeet flying towards the magic door. So he wasn't so stupid after all! He's meandering clumsily around the place, as if he hasn't flown for ages, or perhaps he's just plucked out too many feathers.

'This way, Parakeet!' I shout.

'I'm coming!' he replies.

'Freedom!' I cheer.

'I'm com—'

Suddenly, the magic door closes and Parakeet slams against it. Full throttle. Beak first. You can hear the crunch. And if Gold's right about all animals having souls, then Parakeet's soul must have flown up to heaven in that moment. Though I didn't see it.

Brimstone comes stomping up to the magic door. She looks in bewilderment at the parakeet lying motionless on the ground.

And then at us.

And then back at the parakeet again.

She doesn't compute. Finally, she picks up the parakeet by one of his limp wings using two fingers, carries him at arm's length in front of her and chucks him in the rubbish bin outside the shop.

Afterwards, Gold pops into a human shop for a bit of shopping. Then we sit in the car, and I think about Parakeet meeting his sticky end, and I can't help feeling depressed.

'If she'd at least eaten him,' I sigh. 'But she just chucked him away like dirt.'

'Humans don't eat parakeets,' says Gold.

'No?'

'No.'

'Even so. Poor bugger, that parakeet.'

'Perhaps he wanted to die anyway. I mean, he didn't have the best life,' says Gold.

'Bullshit.'

'He flew straight into the door.'

'That was an accident. No one *wants* to die.'

'Lots of people want to die. And try to kill themselves, too. It's called suicide.'

'Suicide? Bullshit!'

After all, it *is* bullshit. I know lots of dead people, and none of them *wanted* to die. It's just that they were old or sick or both or were eaten or run over or froze to death or starved. That's the way it goes. But if you ask a freezing, starving badger for example: 'Hey, Badger. Wanna die? Fancy committing suicide?' then he's hardly going to say: 'Yeah, why not!' It just doesn't make sense.

What bothers me though is that Gold really seems to believe in this suicide bullshit. I have good instincts and

I can tell he's quite serious. My instinct tells me there's something else going on here, something not quite right about this suicide business and the way Gold talks about it. I start to worry.

But not for long. Because suddenly, the car speeds off and the shaking and roaring starts up all over again. I rest my head on my paws and miaow, remembering to breathe consciously, in and out. And when you're doing all that, you can't think about death at the same time. Otherwise you get in a right muddle. Take it from me.

7. Linda

It could all have worked out so well. And to begin with, I thought it would. I had food to eat, a house to live in, a TV to watch. I even had a bed.

Of course, Gold was always sure to yell, 'Not in my bed, Frankie!' and 'My bed is off limits, Frankie!' and 'Come out of there, Frankie!'

No idea what *off limits* means, mind you. And in any case, humans spend far too much time telling you what *not* to do, if you ask me. Especially when it's something you want to do. Besides, it's a *massive* bed. It would be such a waste to lie in it all on your own, I tell Gold. And I pull out all the stops to win him over: purring, looking cute, stretching . . . the works. Then I try miaowing outside the closed bedroom door at night. Non-stop. It was hard work, but it paid off. Now I sleep in *my* bed every night, which, when he can find space at the edge, Gold shares with me.

And that's what I mean when I say that it all could have worked out so well. I could have lived like a king or a president in the Deserted House. The only spanner in the works was Gold.

The first day after the Pet Shop episode, I'm fed bang on time. Morning, noon and night. But then my bowl starts to be left empty, and food becomes a matter of constant negotiation. When I tell Gold 'I'm hungry!' he says 'I forgot.' Or 'Later, Frankie.' Or 'I just can't right now.'

And yet it's hardly a big ask, is it? Any fool could do it.

As for Gold, he barely eats at all, and one morning he falls off the chair with the bottle of water that isn't water in his hand. He lies on the floor like he's dead, and just as I'm beginning to think he really has died, he opens his eyes and growls, 'Don't look at me like that!'

When he does eat, he doesn't even bother to get out of bed. As soon as he's finished, he dumps the empty and half-empty pans beside the bed. Sometimes I lick them clean. After a while the pans start to smell and, if I'm honest, so does Gold. Being a cat, I have a sensitive nose. Gold smells sour and lonely, like hedgehog breath, and I wish he'd go and take a dip in the lake. Or lick himself clean. But he doesn't lick himself, and he doesn't take a dip, and he doesn't trim the scratchy fur growing on his face.

And there are other typically human things too that Gold doesn't do. Like talking to other humans, for example. Not even on the phone. Nothing like that. And no one ever comes to visit either. Perhaps Gold doesn't have any friends? He doesn't go to work. He doesn't read books. He doesn't listen to music. He doesn't wash the car with a long hose. He doesn't dig around in the garden. He doesn't laugh. He doesn't sit in the sun on a lovely day. Instead, he closes all the curtains and mopes around the house in a sad old coat that he calls a *dressing gown*. It's like living with a corpse, except that Gold isn't dead.

But he's not really alive either. More like a zombie. And that's not the ideal housemate, as I'm sure you'd agree.

The only thing Gold does regularly and seems to enjoy is watching fat people throw arrows at a round board on late-night TV.

And then suddenly, he does something unexpected: he goes out.

'Where are you going?' I ask in amazement.

'To visit someone,' he says.

And so naturally I want to know who this Someone is. Who wouldn't?

To the left of the Big Road lies the rubbish heap. Gold turns right, and I trot along behind him like a dog.

Perhaps it's time I told you what Gold is wearing. He has an old hat on his head, and is wearing a very short pair of trousers – possibly underwear – with his dressing gown over the top, and boots he calls *wellies* on his feet. He's carrying the bottle of water that isn't water in his hand. Even so, the two people we meet along the Big Road just greet him with a polite 'Hello, Mr Gold!' like it's perfectly commonplace here to walk around looking like the village idiot.

Now that Gold has turned right, I have an idea of where he's heading, and soon we come to a field with a fence around it and a lot of fancy stones. Big ones and small ones. And middle-sized ones too.

Gold sits down in front of a small stone under two birch trees at the edge of the field. I sit down next to him.

'This is where she lies,' Gold says after a while. 'Dead and buried. Today is Linda's birthday.'

'Ah,' I say. 'Your wife's under that stone? In the ground?'

Gold nods.

'Must be cold. Dark too. Was your wife very old?'

'No, she wasn't old,' says Gold.

'So how come she's dead?'

'A car accident. She was driving to the shops one morning. She was in the mortuary by the evening. And that was that.'

'I'm sorry.'

'People are always telling me they're sorry.'

'What else should they say?'

'How about: What was she like? Do you miss her? What will you do now?'

Gold turns to the stone. 'Linda, this is Frankie, by the way.'

'Hello, Linda,' I say, raising a paw.

'Frankie's a tomcat. And he speaks. Either that, or I'm crazy. Or drunk. Quite possibly both.'

Gold continues to talk to the stone. He touches it from time to time, as if the stone wasn't a stone.

'Frankie sleeps in our bed too, Linda. I've forbidden him, of course. I know you don't like cats. But it's not my fault. It's just that you're . . . gone. Sitting up there in heaven, laughing at me sharing my bed with a tomcat. But Frankie is warm and he purrs. The only bad news is, he farts as well. My God, you wouldn't believe how he farts! I bet you're laughing now, Linda. I miss that.

I miss everything. Sometimes I find myself following women I meet by chance, in the street, or on a train, in the supermarket . . . anywhere. Women who are wearing your perfume. It drives me crazy. I just can't believe you're dead. I know it, but I don't believe it. Your scent is still in the air. Shit, Linda! You've really done a number on me, you know that?'

Gold starts to cry. It sounds like no animal I've ever heard. And I'd really rather he didn't cry. I nudge him with my nose. I lick his hand. All in vain.

'I haven't brought you anything for your birthday, Linda. I'm so angry with you. Why didn't you . . . why didn't you wait another thirty seconds that day? Why didn't you get into that damned car thirty seconds later? Shit, Linda! My darling. Thirty seconds would have changed everything!'

Then a man walks up to Gold. 'Could you please keep it down a bit? This is a cemetery.'

Gold looks up, points his finger at the man and shouts, 'Shut your mouth!' back.

We sit for a long while in front of the stone without speaking. At one point, Gold jumps to his feet, walks over to another stone, and after looking around, takes the flowers from it and puts them next to Linda's.

'Hey, Gold,' I pipe up after a pause. 'Do you know the joke about the eel and the jackal? The eel says to the jackal: Hey, Jackal . . .'

'What are you doing, Frankie?'

'I'm telling you a joke. To lighten the mood.'

'Bad timing, Frankie. Very bad timing.'

It turns out that humans take death very seriously. Quite personally, in fact. But the truth is, death is only the end of life. Just as birth is the beginning. It's like a sausage. If a sausage didn't have a beginning and an end, it wouldn't be a sausage. And life wouldn't be life. Do you see what I mean?

When we animals die, we just go to sleep somewhere. We lie in the dirt and let the maggots run riot. Sometimes a fox stops by and reads a eulogy.

But humans are different. They build a special sleeping place for their dead, which is very impressive. And they write a bunch of words on the stones. They come and visit the dead, and they tell them stories. The dead couldn't care less, of course. But it's not really about the dead. It's about the living, right?

And I'll tell you something else. Before that day, I'd never spoken to a stone. Or to a dead person like Linda. But at Fatty Heinz's house there's a set of deer antlers directly above the door. I never met their owner when he was a whole deer, bellowing away in the forest, or doing other deer stuff. But now I always stop for a bit of a chat whenever I go past, just so he doesn't feel so lonely hanging there on the wall.

I'll usually ask, 'Hey, Deer, how's it going?'

No reply.

'You're looking good. Nearly rutting time. You ready?'

. . .

True, our conversations are a bit one-sided, but I think he appreciates them all the same. Even if he can't really show it. And to be honest, *I* wouldn't want to be hung up on a wall when the time comes. What a bore that would be. But if I'm being perfectly honest, I wouldn't want to lie here in the sleeping place either, shut up inside a box deep in the ground, with a heavy stone on top of my head, the way humans do it.

'By the way, what are those words on Linda's stone?' I ask Gold on our way back to the Deserted House. I noticed when we were at the sleeping place that there was a lot of writing on all the other stones. But with just three words on it, Linda's was almost bare.

'It says: "See you later,"' says Gold.

'Is that all?'

'That's what Linda said to me. Before she got into the car and never came back.'

See you later.

8. The Meaning of Life

When I wake up the next morning, I'm alone in the bed. I peer around me, ears pricked up. I can hear the roar of a machine in the garden. Then suddenly, everything goes quiet. I hear Gold swearing, then the machine starts roaring again. And so it goes on: Roaring. Silence. Swearing.

At first, I stay put. Because when you're lying in a bed, why would you want to be anywhere else? It's as if, by some powerful magic, you're stuck there. There's nothing you can do about it, that's just the power of the magic at work.

Eventually, I trundle downstairs to the kitchen because I want to know what this *Roaring-Silence-Swearing* business is all about. My new toilet house needs cleaning out: I can tell with a quick sniff. I'm not particularly fond of this odd toilet house, but I like watching Gold clean it. It's quite the show. He crouches down on all fours and fishes out the marbles of poop with a sieve. As if my shit was some priceless treasure.

After a little while, I go out into the garden and have a good stretch. Gold is sitting in the sun sweating and thumping the machine, which has stopped roaring. It's a grass-eating machine and, looking around, I can see it has already had quite a good meal. But now it seems to be tired, or full. In any case, it's no longer making a sound, and Gold is bent over it, swearing.

'Come on, you bastard!' he shouts. 'For the love of God, you bastard, start! Useless piece of—'

And so on.

I find his swearwords a bit lame. I mean, two *bastards* in a row? We animals are much more imaginative: we have swearing down to a fine art. Take bears, for example. Now they *really* have a foul mouth on them. Sheep too. When they go off on one, you'd best shut your ears. But the jewel in the crown – the champions of swearing champions – are magpies.

Magpies are *always* bad-tempered and swear at everyone and everything. They practically consider it a sport. Sometimes when I'm moseying on down through the village with my head in the clouds and I happen across a couple of magpies in a tree – well, then I know I'm in for it. Big time. One of them will shout down, 'Hey, Moggy! You little *cretin*, why don't you piss off!' And the other: 'Give my regards to your mother, and tell her I'll peck her eyes out when I see her!' And then they'll cackle menacingly to each other.

At first, I used to insult them back. But you should never do that with a magpie. It only encourages them. They have this obsession with talking about people's mothers and all the horrors they mean to inflict on them. 'Hey, Moggy, you ugly bastard. I'm going to use your mother's throat as my personal cesspit!' When I heard that one, I thought I'd heard it all. It really knocked me for six. So if you ever meet a magpie and you can hear them shouting at you, just be glad you don't understand them.

I wasn't planning on telling you that story. We animals get a bad enough rap as it is, and I wouldn't want you to think we spend our time flinging foul-mouthed insults around. Now where was I?

Ah, yes! I remember. To return to my story, there I am, relaxing in the sun. I yawn and stretch, and a wind breezes across the lake and dies away again. The wind smells sweet, of water and reeds and fish and earth and home. Clouds float across the sky. I hear grasshoppers hopping. I hear crickets cricketing. It's the most sublime summer's day you could imagine. Or at least, that *I* could imagine.

'Having fun?' I ask Gold, who's still thumping away at the grass-eating machine.

'Fun? Hardly.'

'If you're not having fun, why are you doing it?'

'The lawn has to be mown. And I can't mow the lawn without a lawnmower.'

'Why does the lawn have to be mown?'

'Look at it. The grass is waist high.'

'I like it. You can hide in it.'

'Well, I don't like it.'

'The lawn never bothered you in the slightest all that time you were away. And now it's suddenly started bothering you, so you insist on mowing it and running all across the garden with the machine like an idiot, even though you're having no fun. I don't get it.'

'Don't rile me, Frankie!'

'Just saying . . .'

'Well, sometimes you have to do things you don't enjoy. That's life.'

'That's not my life.'

'So you only ever do things you enjoy?'

'No, not always. Sometimes I also do things I *feel* like doing.'

'Is there a difference?'

'Of course. For example, I *feel* like lying here in the sun. But am I enjoying it?'

'Wow. Very philosophical, Frankie.'

'I agree. It's one of my strengths.' I pause. 'What's *philosophical*?'

Gold stops thumping the machine and looks at me.

'Philosophy is a science that tries to make sense of the world and human existence. Like the meaning of life, for example.'

'There's a meaning to life?'

'Hmm. It's something humans have pondered for a very long time. Whether there is a meaning. And what it might be. All humans seek some purpose in life.'

'I don't.'

'Well, you're a cat. You live by your instincts. We humans are more . . . sophisticated.'

'Does your life have a purpose?'

'Well, I guess that's precisely the problem. It did. But I've lost it.'

'Where?'

'What?'

'Where did you lose your purpose?'

'No idea! It's a figure of speech. It's not about *where*. But *when*. And above all *why*. And at the end of the day, *how*. *How* do you find your purpose again?'

'Now you've lost me.'

'Sorry.'

'I don't think it's for me.'

'What, Frankie?'

'This whole purpose-in-life thing. First you have to *find* it. And then you have to make sure you don't *lose* it. And if you *do* lose it, as you have, then you spend all your time *worrying* about where it's gone. Seems to me the whole business causes nothing but trouble. And then you end up having no time for other things.'

'What other things?'

'You know, important things. Playing, listening to sounds, sniffing around. I like moseying along the Big Road when the tarmac's all nice and warm. Or listening to a bee with its nose stuck in a flower. And then there's a lot of lying in the sun and looking up at the sky to be done too. Like I'm doing right now.'

'You mean, doing nothing.'

'That's not nothing.'

'Well, that's what it looks like.'

'Doing nothing is still *doing*. I'm just not doing *a lot*. And anyway, I'm thinking.'

'Oh? What about?'

'I'm just thinking.'

'Bollocks!'

'If you ask me, you humans just need too much stuff: lawnmowers, toilets, purposes in life and all that jazz.

And where does it get you? Swearing and beating the daylights out of some machine.'

'Don't get me started, Frankie!'

'Look. I'm just saying.'

We fall silent for a while. Then Gold speaks up. 'I just *have* to do something. Anything. Whether it's mowing the lawn or anything else. I need the distraction or I'll go crazy. I can't stand it otherwise.'

'I see.'

'Good.'

'Well, you could clean my toilet out,' I offer. 'If you really *must* do something. To make you feel better.'

'Don't push it, Frankie.'

'Only trying to help. Or you could stroke my fur, if you prefer. On my tummy, or here, under my chin.'

I roll on to my back and expose my tummy and my milk-white chin. Lying like this renders me completely defenceless, and if a hungry eagle were to swoop down from above, it'd be goodbye Frankie. But I'm in the mood for a bit of fuss and attention. And when you're in the mood to do something, you have to do it. Preferably as soon as possible.

'Does fun count as a purpose in life too?' I ask Gold, who, to my surprise, has begun to stroke me. It's a tentative but not altogether bad first attempt. With a bit of practice, he has the potential to be a first-class stroker.

'It counts if you're a hedonist,' he replies. 'For hedonists, the purpose of life is to strive for happiness. For enjoyment.'

'That sounds right up my street! But hang on, I thought I was an agnostic?'

'They're not mutually exclusive. You can be both.'

'Really?'

That clears everything up. Next time someone asks me who I am, I'll reply: 'The name's Frankie. Tomcat, agnostic and hedonist.'

All the stroking makes me sleepy, and silently I thank the Supreme Commander – or whoever had the ingenious idea of giving cats fur to be stroked and humans hands to stroke it. What an inspired idea, Supreme Commander!

After a while, Gold lies down on the grass beside me, looking up at the sky. Now we almost look like *two* tomcats. One small, drowsy one and one big, sad one.

'At the loony bin, we did relaxation exercises every day,' says Gold. 'Meditation too, all that stuff. We had to lie on our backs, like this. With relaxing music playing. I hated it.'

'Loony bin? What's a loony bin?'

'A place for people who are . . . severely unbalanced.'

'Ah, I see.'

And I really did. That humans are unbalanced is as clear as day. For one thing, they have four paws but only walk on two of them. If that's not unbalanced, I don't know what is.

'And in this loony bin you *practised* relaxing?'

'Yes. Doing nothing. Thinking nothing. As a learning exercise.'

This time I know Gold must be lying. Or joking.

Because humans build TVs and enormous buildings and pull off all sorts of other spectacular feats. They wear glasses and trousers and fly around in planes, they know what hedonists are and they know all the other complicated stuff that no one else understands. But you're telling me they don't know how to do nothing?

Ridiculous.

But I say nothing. I don't want Gold to think I don't get the joke, and I don't want to look stupid.

Besides, a startling sound has just caught my attention. And what happens next is more important than anything that's happened so far, even though all that was important too of course. I can hear someone slinking along the Big Road, right up close to the fence where the grass is high. It's a barely audible rustling sound, but my ears are so sharp I can hear when a mole combs his hair or does a tiny fart underground.

I creep towards the fence.

Listening.

Looking.

Listening.

And when I look again, I see the most beautiful molly you can imagine – and that was the start of the whole wretched business.

By the lake, near Fatty Heinz's place, right on the bend in the Big Road, there's a dark red house, and that's where she lives. She hasn't been there long, but when spring came, she suddenly appeared at the window. She was all black with white paws and a little white patch on her back too, like a drop of milk.

Anyway, that was the first time I saw her. And after that I kept on seeing her. I would often steal up to the house in the evening and crouch by the trunk of an old lime tree or hide under a hydrangea. When I caught a glimpse of her sitting in the window, a warm feeling would fill my heart, and when the window was empty, I felt pure misery. I could go on. I could tell you about the charming curl of her tail, or the lovable, languid twitch of her ears. But tragically, the truth of the matter – and the crux of my problem – is, I've never *actually* met her. I know nothing at all about her. Zilch. Zero. Nada. I don't even know her name.

So I decided to invent a nickname for her. To make me feel a bit closer to her, and so that I have something to call her when I'm talking to her in my daydreams.

My first idea was: My Number 1.

Then: My Number 1 For Ever and Ever.

Then: My One. And My Only.

Then: Black Queen of the Window by the Grace of our Supreme Commander.

Then: Kitty Twitchtail.

But all those ideas made me cringe. I mean, Kitty Twitchtail? *Really?* And so I carried on, racking my brains for a super-cool yet truly unique name. And eventually, I found *the one*.

We've had many a conversation in my dreams. She'll start with, 'Hey Frankie! I've heard a lot about you.'

And with a laugh, I'll say, 'Nothing bad, I hope!'

'Oh, on the contrary, Frankie. You're quite the hero round these parts.'

And, with unprecedented modesty, I'll reply, 'Hero, schmero. I just am what I am. D'ya fancy a walk to the lake?'

And she'll sigh, 'I thought you'd never ask.'

And then, I'm like: '. . .'

And she's like: 'Er, Frankie? Hello?'

And I'm like: '. . .'

Total brain fart. Absolute black-out. I was so excited I couldn't utter another word – and that was just in my dream! So you can only imagine how tongue-tied I am this time, seeing her slink across the Big Road like a shadow. And yet, I'm itching to speak to her . . .

I jump up on to the old stone fencepost and gaze after her. Together with Gold, who has come to join me.

'Who's that? Your girlfriend, Frankie?' he asks.

I take a deep breath, my heart racing. Finally, I say to Gold, 'That's *Pussica Purrilenko.*' He's the first to hear my name for her.

And believe it or not, I'd never seriously considered the possibility she could ever be my girlfriend. I mean, not just in my dreams, but in real life. Because Pussica Purrilenko is simply not of this world. Or of any world, for that matter. She's from someplace else. Whereas me? I'm just the tomcat from the rubbish heap.

9. The Worst Feeling in the World

By now, dark clouds have appeared from nowhere. And there's rain coming out of the clouds, big drops of it sploshing down on my head. We dive indoors and I ask Gold if we can watch a film. Something with animals and adventures, as long as it's nothing sentimental. People are always going on about love in sentimental films – 'the Best Feeling in the World', they call it. More like the *Worst* Feeling in the World, if you ask me. Especially when you're all alone and can't help feeling like the biggest coward under the sun. Not to mention the moon and the stars too.

But there's nothing about animals on the TV. Just lots of stuff about humans cooking or sitting on a chair, racking their brains to reply to questions like: *What is the capital of Mauritania? Who was the first man in space? What is the name of the fourth-highest mountain in the world?*

'That's a quiz,' Gold explains.

'Aha! A quiz,' I say.

Though I already know what a quiz is, of course. Old Mrs Berkowitz was always watching quizzes. What I never understood was *why* humans are interested in such things. I mean, *who cares* what the fourth-highest mountain in the world is? I'm sure there must be a *fifth-highest mountain* and a *sixth-highest mountain* too, but what does it matter? The mountain certainly doesn't give a shit. And neither does anyone else. Only humans seem to have this obsession with counting everything. Mountains, rivers, you name it. How high, how long, how wide!

What no one ever asks in the quiz, of course, is whether humans have such huge heads precisely so that they can collect libraries-full of useless information, like what the world's fourth-highest mountain is, for example. Seems a bit like carrying a dung heap on your shoulders.

'Geez, you really need to get your cable TV back up and running,' I say to Gold.

We carry on watching quizzes for a while – *What's the name of the second planet in our solar system? What's an oxymoron?* – and then Gold gets up. He goes upstairs, and after a lot of clattering, he eventually reappears with a dusty machine. 'My old video recorder,' he says. 'And this,' he adds, holding up something black, 'is a video with animals in it. It's all I could find.'

Gold blows the dust off the machine, then he just stands there, staring for ages at the black box. 'Linda . . . she . . . she used to love this film. Sod it: have you ever seen *Lady and the Tramp*?'

I hadn't. But according to Gold, it's an 'absolute classic', so I won't bother getting you up to speed here. Suffice to say it's about two dogs who fall in love. Which, unfortunately, is about the last thing I need right now. Though by the time I realize this, it's too late. I'm already glued to the couch and, with my head in my paws, I let out a sigh. I keep picturing Pussica Purrilenko and me lying next to each other, licking each other clean and bumping our little noses together. If we were in the film of course, that's just how it would be. It would all be so easy, and everyone would be brave and the Tramp would get the Lady. And – even in spite of his ridiculous name – I can't help wishing I was the Tramp right now. Better still, I wish my life were a movie I could live inside. Like, *really* live inside. I'd be Frankie the Hero. There'd be a happy ending every day, and violins would play and everything would be picture-perfect. *That's all, Folks!*

But I don't suppose it's possible to live in a movie. Someone would have already tried to a long time ago if it were.

'Why don't you just talk to her?' Gold asks.

'*Yeah, right.* Pussica Purrilenko? Just, like, *talk* to her. *Sure.*'

'I mean it – you have to do something. It'll only get worse if you don't.'

'Nah.'

'We can go over there together if you'd like, and then you can talk to her.'

'Nooo!'

If I turn up at Pussica Purrilenko's with Gold and his deeply uncool dressing gown at my side, I might as well forget the whole thing.

'C'mon Frankie, what's up?' he says. 'I never realized tomcats were so sensitive in affairs of the heart.'

'You didn't think we were *sensitive*?'

'I mean, don't you just take what you want? Isn't that

how it works with cats? And in all the animal kingdom, generally speaking?'

'Not if you have any class, Gold.'

'And you have class?'

'Absolutely. And anyway, lots of animals aren't who you'd think they are. You know beavers? They mate for life. So do swans. Loyal to the end, they are, even if they are a pompous lot. Or take Victoria penguins. They're always waddling along side by side or standing in front of a hole in the ice freezing their bills off, but they know love when it hits them. Bang! Or storks. Storks spend a lot of time in Africa. Because they have stuff to do there. Business affairs and so on. But every spring they fly right back to their nest to their other halves. And just look at swifts. They even make love on the wing. While looping the loop! A white-knuckle ride if ever there was one. But that's swifts for you! Total adrenaline junkies.'

'How do you know all this?' asks Gold.

'TV. National Geographic.'

'OK. Then go and see this Pussica, take some flowers with you – that's a classy move – and . . .'

'Why flowers?'

'Women like flowers.'

'Human women, maybe. But what's a molly supposed to do with flowers? Eat them? Put them in a tiny little cat vase?'

'OK, OK. My mistake. No flowers. But you must have some kind of traditional courtship ritual, in your world?'

'Well, we break a mouse's neck and leave it in front of the molly's door. That's a classic move. Or we break a bird's neck. Sometimes, a rat's neck . . .'

'Right, I get the point. Break a neck. Very romantic.'

'It's better than flowers.'

'Then go and break a mouse's neck.'

'I can't.'

'Because you feel sorry for the mouse? That's surprisingly decent of you, Frankie.'

'No, because that's what they *all* do! Every tomcat and Harry have tried their luck. Do you know what Pussica Purrilenko's front door looks like? There's a mountain of mice on her step. And next to it a pile of birds. So what, I'm supposed to come along and add another mouse to the pile?'

'I see. You need a real showstopper.'

'Exactly. But what? And besides, I'm terrified. More than I've ever been in my life.'

We sit there for a while, neither of us speaking, and neither of us landing on a showstopping idea. Gold turns the sound up again on the TV. The Tramp says, *Well, hiya, Pidge!* and Lady flutters her eyelashes and swoons in response. Lucky bastard.

'I need to get into television,' I say.

'What?'

Gold turns the sound off again.

'I mean it. When you're famous, like a movie star, it's all dead easy. You just say, I dunno, *pigeon poo* or something and *hey presto*, they all fall in love with you!'

'I wouldn't bet on it, Frankie.'

'Just look at the Tramp!'

'That's a cartoon. Tramp isn't real.'

'Of course he's not real. All right then, take Puss in Boots, for example . . .'

'That's a cartoon too. And a fairytale.'

'Are you telling me . . . Puss in Boots . . . doesn't exist?'

'Yep. He's not real.'

'Are you sure?'

'What about Flipper then? And Lassie? And Fury? Do none of them exist either?'

'No, they exist. They're real animals. Or they were. I'm not sure if they're still alive.'

'See! OK then, look at Flipper, swimming around in his bay. Or wherever he lives. Everyone knows him from the TV. And the lady dolphins – the dolphinettes – well, I bet you any money they're swimming after him like crazy, wanting to touch his fins and making the type of noises that lovesick dolphins do.'

'But you don't become famous just like that. Becoming a movie star is hard work, it takes years.'

'So does love.'

'You'd probably have to go to Hollywood.'

'Where's *Hollywood*?'

'In America.'

'Never heard of it. Is it close to the Pet Shop?'

'It's a bit further away. You have to fly there in a plane or take a ship across the ocean.'

'Are you sure? Perhaps you mean another Hollywood? Mine's just round the corner here. Near the Pet Shop.'

'Frankie, you're riling me up! There's only one Hollywood. In America.'

'*OK, if you say so.* Either way, Hollywood is the best

plan so far. Just imagine me moseying on through the village here, cool as a cucumber and oozing style. And everyone, including Pussica Purrilenko, would stare and shout. "Look, here comes Frankie! Our movie star! Back from Hollywood!" they'd cry.'

Gold looks at me unkindly.

'A movie star, eh? Movie star, my arse. Look at yourself: you're just an ordinary village tomcat. Like I'm just a drunken depressive. Wake up, Frankie, be realistic. You haven't got the guts to talk to some village moggy but you think you can just nip over to Hollywood and become a star. That'll sort everything out. Are you really that stupid, Frankie, or is this just an act?'

And then Gold stops talking and turns up the TV, and I don't say anything either. Instead, I look out of the window, hurt. He'd never spoken to me like that before! And I didn't like that bit about being *realistic* at all. I mean, life and love are hard enough as it is. And just when you've got a good plan together and a bit of hope, these humans come and ruin it all with their talk of reality. I reckon the world would be a lot better off without it.

'So what now?' I ask eventually.

'I can't help you,' says Gold.

'But you had a wife. How did you do it? You must know a good trick.'

'There aren't any tricks in love,' says Gold.

This is disappointing news. Gold's not much use sometimes. But surely every human must have at least one sure-fire love trick up their sleeve?

My problem is that I'm not terribly good at getting to know people. Not just romantically, but generally. That's why I sometimes think I'd like to be a bumblebee. Because bumblebees have no inhibitions whatsoever. They'll talk to anyone, although all that buzzing makes them hard to understand. Bumblebeeish is a language that consists entirely of buzzing. It's quite baffling. But the bumblebee couldn't care less. She just buzzes away at you, convinced that everything she has to say is wildly fascinating and witty. They may be no bigger than a hamster's nose, but they have an ego the size of an elephant. That's just bumblebees for you.

'I wrote to Linda,' Gold suddenly says.

'Huh? I don't understand.'

'Then listen. I was like you once. I couldn't bring myself to talk to her at first. She seemed . . . out of my reach. So I wrote her a letter. With two short poems.'

'And did she like them, the poems?'

'No. She didn't.'

'That's unsurprising.'

'She said she'd never read such pretentious twaddle in her life.'

'Geez, how embarrassing.'

'Oh, yes. Love is embarrassing. You think embarrassing things, say embarrassing things, do embarrassing things.'

'So what happened?'

'A few days later she wrote back saying she'd like to meet a man with the balls to send her such pretentious twaddle. Out of sheer curiosity.'

'She said that? You sent her your pretend-to-waddle and she suggested you meet?'

'Yes. Luckily for me.'

'I just don't get it . . .'

'In love, the first step is to take a chance. Something, *anything*, to get you noticed.'

'What do you mean, get noticed? By writing cheesy poems?'

'If you were a human, I'd say yes, have a go at writing a poem.'

'Very funny,' I say, raising a paw.

But in truth, it wasn't funny at all. Because I do know a poem. One I wrote myself in fact. Not with paw and paper. But it's in my head. And before someone comes to rain on my parade with a 'Get a grip, Frankie!' let me tell you why every word is real and true.

When I used to live with Old Mrs Berkowitz, the radio was always on. Even at night, with the volume turned down, Old Mrs Berkowitz would sleep and I'd sit staring into the darkness. Often there was music playing. But there was a lot of talking too, about humans. Deathly boring stuff. But every so often it wasn't quite so boring. When they read stuff from books. And some of what they read was poetry too. Not that I understood much of it, on account of all the odd words. *Hasten, hasten. Magic's breath. The dear caress. Voice divine*, and all that. But it sounded nice all the same. Like music. Word music. Is that a thing?

Anyway, that's how I first heard poems. And when

I fell in love with Pussica Purrilenko, I sat alone and broken-hearted under my bathtub on the rubbish heap and – with the moon watching me overhead – I decided to write her a poem. *Hasten, hasten. Magic's breath.*

And that's the truth. Cat's honour, I swear.

'Listen, Gold,' I say, sitting up.

'What?'

'I really did write a poem. About love.'

'*You* wrote a poem?'

'Yes. Me. The village moggy. And I've never told anyone else before.'

'Shit, Frankie. Whatever next? Have you written a book too? A play?'

'No. A poem – you do know what a poem is?'

'Yes, I do. But you . . . never mind. Let's hear it.'

'You mustn't laugh! If you laugh . . .'

'I won't laugh. Promise.'

'And no pulling faces either.'

'Absolutely. Straight face.'

'It's my first poem . . .'

I take a deep breath and close my eyes.

For P.P.

I love you so.
My heart sighs
When you're away
But meat pies

Are tastier than peas.
And Emmental's my favourite type of cheese.

I love you so.
What shall I do?
The chicken's sweating in the stew.
A flattened hedgehog thought that he
Would live to be
An OAP.

I love you so.
Do you love me?
My belly's hairy as can be.
You are so fair, we'd make a pair
If you were not so super-cute
Or I not such an ugly brute.

Gold scratches his neck. Then he looks at me, shaking his head. Sometimes he looks as if he's about to say something, but then he just scratches his neck again, like an overgrown monkey. The wait is killing me.

'Well, well,' he says finally. 'You can even rhyme. So what are you waiting for?'

'What do you mean?'

'Look, Frankie. I don't know much about love. But if you're in love and you don't do something about it, you'll regret it. So move your hairy arse and go to her.'

'Nooo! D'you really think I should?'

'Yes, goddammit! And if she doesn't like your poem, then she hasn't got a heart anyway.'

'It *is* rather good, isn't it? Does this make me a real poetician?'

'It sure does, Frankie.'

And I think Gold really meant it. At least I hope so. Because I've never seen anyone conquer a heart just like that – and a cold one at that – all thanks to a poem. And I can't imagine it either. But since I didn't have any other showstoppers up my sleeve, I had no choice.

10. Fancy a Nut?

I took ages about it, walking in zigzags and sniffing around aimlessly. A couple of times, I nearly lost my nerve and turned tail. When I finally find myself in front of the dark red house, there's no one at the window, and my first feeling is one of relief. But it doesn't last . . . A wave of longing surges through my heart, and then I'm suddenly thrown into despair. Is this normal? Is this love? Are my emotions supposed to be all over the place?

I crouch by the trunk of the old lime tree, growing sadder and sadder. So wrapped up am I in gloomy thoughts and despair that I don't notice a rustling in the treetops above me. Someone whizzes down towards me like greased lightning, and I nearly jump out of my skin when the Someone hollers: 'Frankie! Hey! I'm here!'

Looking up, I see a small brown face with big ears. Upside down, and staring straight at me.

'Shit, Muscles Nutkin, you scared the life out of me!'

The face's owner jumps down from the tree, exclaiming excitedly: 'Frankie, old mate!'

'Muscles, old mate!' I reply.

'Man, it's great to see you!'

'Yeah, man! Great!'

He bumps foreheads with me and we cross tails. Then

we bump foreheads again. And noses. Then we start all over again.

This went on for some time. I was really pleased to see Muscles. I don't have many friends, you see. Only two, to be precise. And Muscles Nutkin is one of them.

I know you humans like to have a lot of friends. I've seen films where they throw these huge parties. In one, this human invites a massive crowd over who are all supposed to be his friends. But I don't believe it for a second. All those people just came for the food. I know as well as most that real friends are incredibly rare, and sometimes you can't find any at all, and then you're all alone in the world. That thought really scares me: the idea of being alone in the world, I mean. Being alone means spending all day talking to yourself, resigned to the terrible fate of licking your fur and your arse without any company. Nothing but arse-licking and loneliness. So I know I'm lucky to have two friends, even though I sometimes think three would be even better. Good to have an insurance policy. You know . . . just in case one of them kicks the bucket.

For a while I was also friends with a sheep called Attila the Hun. Or rather, I fantasized that I was. But it's not easy being friends with a herd animal.

I would go out into the fields and say: 'Hey, Attila the Hun. How's it going? What's for lunch? Grass again?'

And Attila would gawp at me and reply, 'I'll have to ask the herd.'

Or I'd say, 'Hey, Attila, coming to the lake?'

'I'll have to ask the herd,' would come the reply.

Or I'd say: 'Hey, Attila, when you need a crap, do you have to . . .'

'I'll have to ask the herd,' he'd nod.

I think that's why our friendship never took off. Some days, I wish I had a herd like that to look out for me and think for me. Because all the thinking and deciding for yourself can really knock the wind out of you, you know. This whole life business can just be a bit exhausting sometimes.

'Frankie, old mate. What ya doin' here?' asks Muscles Nutkin, sitting down next to me in the shade of the old lime tree.

'Me? Nothing. Thinking.'

'Fancy a nut? They're good for your brain.'

'No, thanks, you're all right.'

'I think you could do with a nut. What's on ya mind?'

'Oh, you know, this and that.'

'Ah. So it's a molly on your mind then.'

'No! Why?'

I don't want to talk about Pussica Purrilenko. What we have is my secret. Because there's nothing more ridiculous than a lovesick tomcat.

'You look so depressed.'

'That's how I always look, Muscles.'

'No, really. You look like a magpie's crapped on your head, if you ask me.'

'Well, I didn't ask you, did I?'

'Ooh, you're in a mood, mate. Sure you don't fancy a nut? Where've you been all this time, anyway? Me and the Prof were getting worried.'

That had even crossed my mind. So much had happened since I'd last seen my friends. And they knew nothing of my new life that had begun the day I saw Gold playing with the string hanging from the ceiling.

'Sorry,' I say. 'I'll tell you all about it in a moment. Honestly, you'll be amazed! Will you fetch the Professor?'

'Right you are, Frankie,' he replies, shooting back up the old lime tree in the blink of an eye and disappearing into the treetops. I barely have time to cast a glance at the dark red house, where the window's still empty, before Muscles Nutkin is back. He shimmies on down the tree trunk, calling to me that the Professor is on his way.

He's not even out of breath. But that's Muscles Nutkin for you. It's not for nothing we call him that. And he doesn't have another name either, in case you were wondering. Word on the street is that his real name is Uwe or Bernd or something equally soul-destroying. But like I said, they're just rumours. Muscles has grown amazingly fit from all that climbing up and down trees, and he's not shy about his muscles either. 'I *want* to be objectified, Frankie,' he'll say. I think humans would use the term 'gym bro'? Hence the moniker.

And then we see the Professor approaching. You can spot him a mile off, hobbling along the Big Road. The Professor is really ancient and has extremely short, sausage-like legs. He's a dachshund, you see, and the Supreme Commander (or whichever higher power you report to) has decreed that all dachshunds should have short sausage-like legs and their bellies should almost scrape the ground. Why? I don't know. Stuff like that is above my pay grade. And perhaps the Supreme Commander (or whoever) doesn't know either. After all, there are so many different kinds of animal legs, on giraffes, woodpeckers, bumblebees, camels, tortoises, skunks, bats, and so on. I can't possibly imagine how the Supreme Commander (or whoever) managed to keep an eye on the bigger picture and decide fairly who got what, back in the days when animals were first puzzled together.

The Professor's legs aren't just extremely short, though. There are also too few of them – at least for a dog, anyway. There's one leg missing, you see, in his front left-hand corner. So you can just imagine how long it takes this positively prehistoric, three-legged dachshund to reach us. Even snails move faster.

And look, here I hold my paws up. I know full well that dachshunds are dogs, and that means they are leash animals. And you know what I think about dogs: I have some . . . reservations. I am a cat of rock-solid principles after all, and a cat is nothing without his convictions! But sometimes, just sometimes, you have to be flexible. Otherwise principles are no fun, and they make life terribly complicated.

Besides, I've never seen the Professor on a leash. He lives with Mr Adam, who is equally ancient and walks hunched over. Houses could be built in the time it takes for the two of them to hobble along side by side through the village. Trust me when I say there is no need for a leash to hold the Professor back.

*

'Evening, gentlemen,' says the Professor when he finally arrives, nodding his greying head with his usual formality.

'Frankie, my boy.' A nod.

'Muscles Nutkin.' Another nod.

Then he lies down with a grunt under the old lime tree and closes his eyes. After a while, just when I think he must have dropped off, he says hoarsely, with his voice barely a whisper: 'Now, Frankie, my boy. What happened to you? Tell us all about it. My old ears are open wide.'

And so I tell them the whole story: about Gold, the Deserted House I'm living in now, the woman with the briefcase, the Pet Shop, Brimstone, the crazy parakeet, Hollywood, and how I suddenly became an agnostic and a hedonist.

I embellish the story ever so slightly here and there, and when I get to the end I'm fully expecting my friends to congratulate me on my new life. Something like: 'Wow, Frankie! Gotta hand it to you – you've done really well for yourself. We're so proud of you.'

But no one says a word. Muscles Nutkin just stares at me. The Professor utters a faint groan.

'What's up, friends?' I ask, after a pause.

'You're living with a human?' Muscles Nutkin retorts. He spits the word *human* out like it's a disease. 'I expected more from you, Frankie. I thought you were a free animal!'

'I'm still a free animal.'

'Not if you're living with the human you're not.'

'Nonsense,' I say. 'Being a free animal is a state of mind, amigo.'

'No, Frankie. Living with a human makes you dependent. You lose all your auto—auto— oh, you know. Your auto-thingummy . . . !'

'He means your autonomy,' says the Professor, flatly.

'Exactly!' says Muscles Nutkin.

'Are you out of your mind?' I exclaim.

'I have only two words to say, Frankie: "It's an utter disgrace!"'

'That was four.'

'Was it? Well, let's make it five then: "Traitor!"'

'And that was one. Here's a thought: if maths isn't your forte, how about you stop telling me in advance how many words you're planning on saying?'

Muscles Nutkin scratches his head.

'But do you really want to get fat, Frankie?'

'What?'

'You get fed every day. Served on a plate, right? Before you know it, you'll lose all your natural instincts, my friend. You'll get lazy. And your mind'll turn to mush too, you know. Look at me, Frankie: this impossibly muscular body, this nimble mind – all that goes away when you shack up with a human.'

'Well, don't you worry. I won't get fat.'

'You already have put on a bit of weight, if you ask me.'

'No, I haven't!'

'And what's this then, hmm?' says Muscles Nutkin, poking me in the tummy.

'Stop poking me!' I screech.

'See? Love handles! They may be cute now, but just you wait. You'll be round as a ball before you know it.'

'Up yours!'

'Where's your collar anyway, Frankie?'

'Haven't got one!'

'I bet you have. One with bells on? Here comes our Frankie! You can't miss him! Living with the human now too. Sits up and begs on command. Tinkle, tinkle!'

'I'm warning you, Nutkin!'

'Put a sock in it, you two!'

This from the Professor, who's just lying there, peering through droopy eyelids. Even though he can only speak in a hoarse whisper these days, he still manages to sound incredibly stern, speaking with the authority of a president or a mafia boss on TV. I don't know how he does it. That's his secret. In any case, it does the trick. We both fall silent.

'Now say sorry! Go on!'

We shake paws, bump noses, bump heads.

'Hey, I'm sorry Frankie. It's just . . . I'm really worried. You're living with a human! D'ya fancy a nut, by the way?'

'No, thanks. Maybe later.'

'You're sure? I've got some fabulous nuts, you know! Hazelnuts, walnuts, corn kernels, acorns, spruce seeds . . . Go on, have a nut!'

Once, in the early days of our friendship, I actually said yes to this. Just to be nice. Nuts are obviously not my thing. It was winter, and we trudged around for ages looking for this one particular nut. Every couple of seconds, Muscles Nutkin would cry out, 'Here it is!' but there was never anything there. In the autumn, he buries nuts obsessively all over the place. 'You have to plan ahead, Frankie. Always plan ahead!' But before long, he forgets where he's hidden them. Because there are just too many hiding places. He may have drive, but he's not so hot on logistics. So we ended up freezing our butts off in the snow. Scuttling from one place to the next, he would shout, 'Here it is, Frankie! Or is it? I can't remember. Is it here?' before moving on to the next. He was at his wits' end.

The thing is, Muscles Nutkin is a forward-planning animal who's constantly worrying about the future. He can't help it. That's just his nature. And some humans are the same. Old Mrs Berkowitz was never satisfied until she'd lugged all these heavy potatoes down to her cellar: 'Better safe than sorry,' she used to say. But you already know what happened to her. She keeled over and was carted off in the white car. And who knows what became of her potatoes! So, for what it's worth, I don't think much of all this forward planning. A wolf might catch me tomorrow, and then it's game over for Frankie. And I'll be left thinking: *drat*, if only you hadn't spent your life burying nuts or potatoes or whatever, and had a bit more fun instead. At least that's what *I'd* be thinking. After all, a corpse has no use for a stockpile of nuts.

The Professor turns on to his side with a groan, complaining about how the hot weather's afflicting him and how the summers used to be so much cooler and wetter, and how things were better all round in 'the old days'. Then he opens his dark, watery dachshund eyes for a moment and looks at me. Looking back at him, I'm reminded that the Professor's like a father to me. Or rather a grandfather.

'Listen to me, Frankie, my boy. Are you listening to me?'

'Of course, Professor.'

'You have to remember: humans are fickle, unpredictable creatures. My first human beat me half to death with a spade. That's how I lost my leg. My second human, Mr Adam, took me in. I'm a useless, three-legged dachshund who can't get down a badger's den any more. He carries me up the stairs and even sings me a silly little song on my birthday. The man's hardly Sinatra and he can't carry a tune, but fortunately for us both, I'm hard of hearing. And at the end of the day, he's the best of humans, and I'd bite anyone who tried to do him harm. If I still had all my teeth, that is. What I'm saying is, it's important to pick the right human, Frankie. Is Gold the right human for you?'

The Professor creeps closer and holds out his stump to me. Right under my nose.

'Look, Frankie. Take a good look at my stump.'

I give it a quick glance. Fond as I am of the Professor, it sometimes freaks me out that he's only got three legs. I once dreamt that his fourth leg was walking through the woods looking for him, and I tried to explain to the leg where he lived, but it couldn't hear me. And then it got terribly angry and tried to kick me, and I scarpered through the woods with the Professor's leg in hot pursuit.

'Look closely!' said the Professor, waving his stump.

'I *am*!'

'What do you see?'

'A stump?'

'The *truth*, Frankie. This stump reminds me to be on my guard at all times. The human is the worst animal on the planet. Look at my stump!'

After making me promise no less than five times to always be on my guard, the Professor finally stops pointing it at me and says quietly: 'I know your human.'

'Gold?'

'Yes, Richard Gold, the writer. Poor devil.'

'His wife's dead.'

'I know, Frankie.'

'No shit?!'

That just sort of slipped out. The Professor raises a conciliatory paw.

'It was in the paper, Frankie. A car accident. Down at the bottom of the village, where the Big Road joins the motorway. That's where it happened. Did you know I read the newspaper? And books, too.'

Muscles Nutkin rolls his eyes.

'Yes, Professor. I know.'

Here we go again . . .

The Professor is very smart, in fact he's the smartest animal I know – partly because of all the newspapers and books he reads, I guess. But who knew smart people had to spend so much time telling you they're smart?

'They both died in the accident. The wife and the child,' says the Professor, breaking into a howl and a soft *a-wooo.*

'What child?' I ask.

'The wife was due a pup.'

The wind played in the old lime tree as we lay there in the twilight, just dozing and doing nothing in particular, the way you can with your friends. Nearby I could hear Fatty Heinz panting after his stick. Eventually, the last ray of light disappeared over the lake and we bade each other goodnight. Muscles Nutkin raced off into the treetops, and I wandered back along the Big Road with the Professor.

'Tell me about Gold,' the Professor says.

'We talk a lot,' I say.

'Humanish?'

'Yes. Unavoidable, I'm afraid.'

'Frankie, have you forgotten the *Three Golden Rules*?'

'Yeah, yeah, I know. Rule One: act stupid. Rule Two: act stupid. Rule Three: act stupid. Like you're at their mercy. But I just sort of . . . fell into it.'

'That's no good, Frankie. Now he knows what you're capable of. *And* Gold is a male. The females are gentler. With males you have to show them straightaway who's the leader of the pack. How old is he?'

'No idea. Around middle age?'

'That's good. Young humans are too wild. What are his teeth like?'

'I didn't notice.'

'Teeth are important, Frankie. Is he a good eater?'

'He eats, yes. But mostly he drinks.'

'And his fur? Is it glossy?'

'Hmm, he doesn't have much fur. Just a bit on his head.'

'Aha, middle-aged male. Not much fur. What about walkies?'

'Not keen. Spends a lot of time sitting around. Brooding. He's a sad man, and angry with the world.'

'He needs exercise, Frankie. Get him out whatever the weather! I know you young'uns have new-fangled ideas about discipline. But you can't afford to be blasé, a human needs clear signals. Guidance. Otherwise he'll become a nuisance to all other creatures. Does he groom himself?'

'Not much. He just acts . . . weird. He talks weird. Says he's lost his purpose in life and stuff like that.'

'That's good news, Frankie. Don't you see? Now *you're* his purpose in life. He just doesn't know it yet.'

Suddenly, I felt the weight of the world on my shoulders. I mean, I've never been anyone's Purpose in Life before. At least, not that I know of. And the idea of becoming the Purpose in Life for a big grown man like Gold, just like that, with no prior experience to speak of . . . Well, it seemed a huge responsibility. And I don't really *do* responsibility.

'I never thought it would be this difficult,' I sigh.

'Yes, humans are a lot of work, Frankie. But handled well, they can bring some joy, you know. Humans think they're clever, and we let them believe it. We play our part, but secretly we're the ones calling the shots. Humans are happier that way. And if your human's happy, you're happy. You see? In academic circles, we call that *dialectics*, my boy.'

But before I can ask the Professor what *dialectics* are, he's already slipped through the wide bars of the fence and is hobbling up the path to his house. Suddenly, he slows right down, growing wobblier with each step. And then I realize: he's putting on a show. He has a plan.

Finally he sits down and lets out a short bark. Mr Adam scuttles to the door, his voice heavy with concern: 'Oh Barney, dear chap. Wait, I'm coming! Don't you worry!' Then he picks the Professor up with a grunt and carries him into the house. The whole charade is quite a spectacle to behold.

You have to hand it to the Professor. He's a virtuoso at this dialectics business.

I carry on to the Deserted House, wondering what, as Gold's new Purpose in Life, I should do next. Or *ought* to do next. Or whether, as someone's Purpose in Life, you're supposed to just continue on in your own merry way, taking things as they come.

I'm so lost in thought that I don't notice the car at first. A small white car, parked outside the Deserted House. And I can already hear that familiar field-sparrow cheep. I feel sick with shock and dive into a bush, convinced that my thumping heart can be heard from miles around. Luckily, human ears are no good for anything except scratching.

Standing in the garden is Anna Komarova, with her briefcase. I think of the vicious arrows, the stuff that burns, and then in a flash, I remember that she was going to pop in to check up on me. Gold is standing next to her.

'Frankie! Frankie, you've got a visitor!' he calls out.

Why do humans always expect you to come running the minute they call?

I lie there in the bushes, just a few tail lengths away, and wait. Ideally, Anna Komarova will get straight back into her car, disappear and never come back. But that's not what happens.

At first, the two of them stand side by side without speaking. Then Anna Komarova says something about the weather and how warm it is at the moment, and Gold says something about the weather and how warm it is at the moment. And then Anna Komarova asks after me.

'How's my little Pooshock? Is the wound healing OK?' she says.

'The wound? Oh yes. I think it's all fine,' says Gold.

'But you don't know?'

'Oh yes. Frankie told me himself. *I can report that my head is healed!* Those were his words.'

'Ha *ha.* Very funny. And where is he now?'

'Out and about. He wrote a poem and wanted to read it to his lady love.'

'You're quite the comedian, aren't you? Are you drunk? I can smell the fumes from here, if I may say so.'

'Now see, *that's* what I like about you. You're always so direct. Why don't you join me? Could I interest you in a vodka?'

'No, thank you. I'm on duty.'

'As a Russian, I half expected you to be less restrained.'

'I'm from Kyrgyzstan.'

'Ah well, whatever. It's all the Soviet Union to me.'

'So what is it you do here all day, then?' asks Anna Komarova. 'Apart from drinking yourself to sleep, I mean.'

'Thinking. *Ruminating*. Mowing the lawn. Buying cat food. Waiting for the day to pass. Oh yes, and the aforementioned drinking too, of course.'

'I see . . . You're unemployed.'

'I take issue with that. I'm not unemployed. I'm a writer.'

'Oh, a *writer?*'

'What's that supposed to mean?'

'What's *what* supposed to mean?'

'*Oh, a writer?* The ironic tone.'

'All I said was: "Oh, a writer."'

'There you go again!'

'My God, aren't you sensitive! What sort of stuff do you write then? Whodunnits?'

'No, novels. Proper literature.'

'Shame. I like whodunnits.'

'Is that all you read?'

'Yes, and thrillers.'

'You're welcome to borrow one of my books. As a *writer*, it's my job to educate, after all. You might like it.'

'Hmm. Or perhaps I won't. Does anyone die in your book?'

'Yes.'

'Well, that's a good start. I won't touch a book where no one dies. But I will be honest with you. You should know, I *will* tell you if it's boring. And I won't finish it if I don't like it. Title?'

'What?'

'What's your book called?'

'*My Summer with Emily*.'

'Seriously?'

'Don't you like it?'

'Sounds pretty cheesy to me.'

'It's a classic, actually. There's a difference.'

'It sounds like the sort of book an old lady in some humdrum English village would read – the kind of woman who eats egg-and-cress sandwiches and writes novels about other women who also eat egg-and-cress sandwiches and are hopelessly, desperately, *embarrassingly* in love with some lord or duke.'

'An interesting analysis.'

'I bet *My Bloody Summer with Emily* would have sold far better. Or perhaps, *The Emily Files*.'

'Next time I'll consult you first.'

'Do. Oh, before I forget: I've found someone for little Pooshock.'

'Found someone?'

'A nice family willing to take him in. Weren't you keen to get rid of him?'

'Was I? I don't remember.'

'For a writer you have a remarkably bad memory.'

'Frankie's staying here with me. He *needs* me.'

'Of course. He needs you.' She let out a laugh.

'What's so funny?'

'Nothing. Nothing at all. I just think maybe it might be the other way round.'

'Nonsense.'

'Listen, I think I'll just wait here another quarter of an hour for little Pooshock to come back so I can take a look at his wound. Perhaps he'll turn up. Is that OK?'

'No.'

'No?'

'Only if you'll have a vodka with me.'

'Oh for God's sake, you really are an arsehole.'

'Yes. I know.'

I watch Gold go inside and fetch a bottle and two glasses. I hear a clink, then they carry on talking. After a while, Gold goes to fetch two chairs and they carry on talking. And talking. *And talking*. Anna Komarova laughs a couple of times, and then they carry on talking some more.

It's almost unbearable.

No one calls out for me again. And even though I wouldn't have come, it's nice to feel wanted sometimes.

I slip away to the Big Road, thinking of Gold's words. *Frankie's staying here*. I grin to myself at the thought. Somewhere in that cold heart he must have some feelings for me after all!

I don't really know where to go after that, so I amble down to the lake and find a quiet spot to sit by the water. The place echoes with human voices: I can hear nearly every word, even from the opposite shore. It really is amazing how sound carries over water at night. There are two boats on the lake: one of them passes close to me, and I think how strange it must be to sit in a boat with nothing beneath you but black water, floating right over the heads of all the fish.

And then I leave the lake and make my way up the mountain, through the dark, humanless world. A half-moon hangs above me, and I shout up to it.

'Hello, Moon. Getting fatter too, I see. Good to see you though, old pal.'

Bats are squeaking, hedgehogs snuffling. I can smell raccoon poo, I can smell the dusty summer cornfields, and I wonder whether Pussica Purrilenko is in her window right now, and I wonder why I was born such a coward. I feel positively wretched.

At the top of the mountain, I curl up under my old bathtub and gaze into the moonlight until I begin to dream. Most dreams are twaddle, if you ask me. They make no sense, and whenever you tell someone about them you sound like you've lost the plot. That's why I never tell anyone about my dreams.

But this time I dreamt about Hollywood. And as the humans are always saying, dreams can come true.

11. Hollywood

When I'm back in the Deserted House, I notice some sudden changes. And as always with sudden changes, it's hard to make head or tail of them at first, and you find yourself in a constant state of bewilderment. But I'm getting ahead of myself.

Sometime after that curious evening with Anna Komarova, I hear Gold whistling a tune. I don't know which tune, and in any case, it doesn't matter. But when I see him standing there in the kitchen whistling, I can only gawp in disbelief. Another day passes and he draws back all the curtains, with sunlight suddenly streaming into the Deserted House. I blink and squint. Then he clears away the smelly pans, and one day he's on the phone for ages talking to another human (no idea who, he refuses to tell me), and in quite a pleasant tone too, mind. By that I mean there's almost no swearing. What really floors me though is when, one morning, he suddenly casts off his miserable and dishevelled dressing gown and starts wearing the sort of thing a normal person might wear. *You know what I mean*. He looks . . . presentable? I hardly recognize the Gold I used to know. But guess what? On one of these gobsmacking, change-filled days, Gold turns to me and says with a smile, 'Get in the car, Frankie. We're going to Hollywood.'

I don't, of course, because I'm convinced he's talking utter bullshit again, as he's known to do. Besides, the last car journey we went on was quite enough for a lifetime. But he insists, telling me that we are in fact going to Hollywood. To something called *casting*, whatever that is.

'And what about realism?' I ask.

'What about it?' Gold replies.

'A few days ago, you said I should forget about Hollywood. Because I'm just an *ordinary village moggy*. And now we're suddenly going to Hollywood after all?'

'Frankie, I'm just doing you a favour. We're going on an adventure, OK? And I'm really sorry to break it to you, but that doesn't mean you're going to be movie star. It's not realistic. In fact, it's very, very, very unrealistic.'

But at the words *movie star* I decide to get in the car after all. Because the way I look at it, as long as you believe in something and you can picture it in your head, then it's realistic. That's just my humble opinion. And I can picture Hollywood only too clearly. Being welcomed with open paws by a group of waving and cheering humans, all crying out to me, 'Hey, Frankie! There you are at last!'

'Did you have a good trip?' they'll ask. 'Here, have a bite to eat first and a rest, then we'll make you a *star*. It won't take a minute. How does that sound?'

I reply with a casual but confident, 'Sounds good to me, my friends.'

We drive on past meadows and fields, and when I look back, the village has disappeared. How long we're on the road, I don't know. But believe me: you don't need to fly across the sky to get to Hollywood. Or cross the ocean in a ship. We just turned left at the Pet Shop, then right, then straight on, then right again, and then Gold pulls out a scrap of paper with the Hollywood address pencilled on it.

After a while, we see mountains looming ahead. We're driving straight towards them. But as we get closer, it turns out they're not mountains after all, but huge towers and soaring buildings. They're growing out of the ground and they all look the same. And I mean *exactly* the same. Like a herd of zebras.

'That's the city,' says Gold.

One of the towers, the tallest of them all, has a spike on top, and the spike is in a cloud: I've never seen anything like it, and suddenly I'm very aware of how small I am. I'm a metaphorical flea in the fur coat of life.

'That's the city?' I mew weakly, shrinking back into the car seat. Next to the tower with the spike on top is a high building with big, illuminated red letters on it. And that's where we're heading.

'What do the letters say?' I ask Gold.

'Happy Cat,' he says.

But in front of the building is a road we have to cross on foot, and I'm terrified we'll never make it. So. Many. Cars. So many humans. And they're all running to some other place in the city. I can't for the life of me work out why. Is it fear? Or hunger? Or perhaps they're in pursuit of their prey. All of them are talking into their tiny telephones. Whenever a human is called by one of these telephones, they have to answer it. They have no choice, because the telephones control everything and humans obey them like dogs. Some humans have food in their paws, too. Bread rolls and sausages, and so on. They're running and eating at the same time, no doubt for fear that another human will snatch it from them before they can get it to safety. Good thinking!

Gold lifts me on to his shoulder and carries me across the road to the building with the illuminated letters.

'Are we in Hollywood now?' I ask as we enter the big foyer.

'Sort of,' says Gold.

An old man dressed all in black comes up to us.

'Casting?' he asks. 'Elevator, second level down.'

Then we go underground like moles. But it doesn't look anything like a mole's home here. I know one, you see. He's called Digby, and Digby's place is dead gloomy. I had a peep inside it once: it's basically just a tunnel brimming with old earthworms and snails. I wouldn't say it has *ambience*. Mod cons and interior design aren't really a mole's forte. They're poor blighters, if you ask me.

When we reach the place called S*econd Level Down*, the door opens. We step out into a hall *full* of cats. Mollies and toms everywhere you look, sitting on chairs with their humans or standing in a queue or walking around on a leash or staring through the bars of a basket. I follow Gold to a long table where two humans are sitting. A woman and a man. I guess they work for Hollywood. The woman has sharp red claws and the man has no fur on his head. Gold fishes out a scrap of paper from his bag.

'It says here you're looking for a cat for a promotional film? This is Frankie,' he says, gesturing to me. 'He's the best.'

And even though it's the plain and obvious truth, I still appreciate Gold for mentioning it.

The two humans behind the desk look at me. Then they look at Gold. The man with the furless head points to me and says, 'What *on earth* is *that*?'

'Pardon?' says Gold.

'That straggly creature there? Did you find it in the gutter?'

'No, not exactly on the street. It's a long story,' Gold replies.

'What's it supposed to be?'

'Well, he's a tomcat, *obviously*.'

'Yes, but what breed?'

'What breed? No idea. Does it matter what breed?'

'Of course it matters. Look around you,' the man says, gesturing across the room. 'See those cats at the back there? They're pure-bred Siamese. And over there is an Egyptian Mau, and these here are Chinchilla cats. Over there are Sacred Birmans, Russian Blues, Maine Coons and an exquisite Turkish Van.'

'Turkish Van?' Gold laughs. 'Lowered suspension, extra-wide tyres, chrome exhaust pipe?'

The man doesn't laugh.

'Your cat . . .'

'His name's Frankie.'

'Your cat looks like a bog-standard, run-of-the-mill house cat with God knows what mongrel ancestry.'

'So what?'

'We're looking for a star. Not a black sheep.' This from the woman with the red claws sitting next to him behind the desk.

The man clears his throat and says to Gold, 'Look, I'm sure your cat is . . . a colourful specimen. But he is very ordinary. Bordering on ugly, even. And we're casting for Happy Cat Sauce Supreme. The Number One in cat foods. We're looking for the new face of their brand!'

'But he has the perfect Sauce Supreme face,' says Gold. 'Frankie likes sauce.'

'What happened to his left ear?' asks the man. 'There's a whole chunk missing. We can't take some battered, bitten old creature here. God forbid!'

Suddenly, the woman behind the desk pipes up, looking straight at me. 'Wait a minute. I know, I know. This might sound crazy. But look at him. He has something. A kind of . . . authenticity.'

'Authenticity?' The man sounds surprised.

'You know. There's a real aura of uncouth individuality about him. What with the half an ear as well. He's . . . alternative. Don't you think?'

'And that's a good thing?'

'Exactly. All we have to do is create the right narrative. I mean: here's a tomcat who looks like a million other cats. A moggy from the street. A wretched mongrel. What's more, he's only got half an ear. He can barely hear what's going on around him any more, he struggles to find his way around, he's excluded from society. But he never gives up. He fights for respect and love! People are moved by stories like that. And it would be totally in keeping with the zeitgeist: Happy Cat Sauce Supreme – we embrace *all* cats . . . Is there anything else we can use for his sob story?'

'He doesn't have a sob story,' says Gold.

'Of course not,' says Red Claws. Then she takes a photo of me, writes something on a big piece of paper, gives it to Gold and says, 'Welcome to the casting auditions for Happy Cat Sauce Supreme.'

I couldn't follow all the human talk at Hollywood. I only kept up for about half of it. Or half of half of it.

'What *is* casting, anyway?' I ask Gold.

'Well, it means they're going to see if you're right for the role.'

'But am I? They said I'm ugly.'

'You're not ugly, Frankie. Well, perhaps you are a bit. But you have charisma.'

And believe it or not, I've never actually thought about how I look. And I've never thought about how other animals look either. Whether they're beautiful or ugly. Except Pussica Purrilenko, because she's something else entirely. Out of this world. Some animals are stupid arseholes, of course. Raccoons, for instance. But I couldn't tell you whether they were ugly. Just that they're arseholes, if you see what I mean.

Humans aren't like that. They're always talking about what people look like or what they *are*. And they make such a huge deal of it. *Hey, Frankie, you're ugly! Hey,*

Frankie, you're a mongrel! Hey, Frankie, you've only got half an ear! And another thing humans always want to know is how old a person is. They go *on* and *on* about it. But what does it matter how old you are? As long as you're alive.

Take a hot tip from a tomcat who's been around the block a bit: forget all that nonsense and believe me when I say that the world is divided only into arseholes and non-arseholes. You're one or the other, simple as that. The only question is, how do you tell the arseholes from the non-arseholes? That part's not so easy. You humans would be better off focusing more of your energy on that.

Now then. All this thinking and dispensing advice to humanity has made me hungry.

'Got anything to eat?' I ask Gold.

'No, sorry, Frankie.'

'I thought there'd be food and everything at Hollywood?'

'They tend not to eat so much in Hollywood,' says Gold.

And so I mooched around the hall in search of food. We had to wait about for ages for the casting auditions, so I had time to kill. Second hot tip of the day: if you ever go to Hollywood, remember to take some grub with you and something to play with, or a Hollywood film. Otherwise you'll die of boredom.

'Hey, kid! Psst! Over here.'

At first I can't tell who's speaking. Then, a few tail

lengths away, I see a molly winking at me and whispering behind her paw. 'Psst! Over here, kid!'

So I go over to her, thinking it'd be good to know someone in Hollywood and have a few connections. You know, network. The molly in question is sat in a huge basket. There's a grid at the front, and she slips her paws through it.

'Hey, kid! Psst! Got any?'

'What?'

'I said, have you got any? Come on, give it here.'

'What do you mean?'

'Don't act dumb – spare a bit for an old lady.'

'But I haven't got anything. Have you? I'm hungry.'

'Oh, come on! It doesn't have to be a lot. But I need a bit. I need the good stuff.'

'The good stuff?'

'Oh, shit! You really haven't got anything, have you? Why do I always pick the wrong guy? It never used to be like that. Back in the day I had a sense for these things. They were all crazy about me.'

'I'm Frankie,' I say, because I don't know what else to say.

'I'm Bianca von Hosenwalde-Wolfenstein. And your name's Frankie? *Just* Frankie?'

'Frankie . . . von Rubbish-Heap-Mountain,' I reply.

'OK, Frankie von Rubbish-Heap-Mountain. This your first time? Sure looks like it.'

'Yes. I've only just arrived in Hollywood.'

'*Hollywood?* No wonder. Have you any idea what goes on here, kid?'

'Well, I want to be a movie star. For love's sake.'

'A romantic. How sweet.'

And then she fixes me with a stare. They make me quite dizzy, those narrow, incredibly blue eyes glinting at me from her dark face. It's a little unnerving. I've never seen a cat like Bianca von Hosenwalde-Wolfenstein before.

'Stick with me, kid. I'm the star around here. Good ol' Bianca will look out for you, OK?'

'Are you a *breed*?' I ask. It's a word I've just heard the humans using.

'Of course I'm a breed, kid. Pure Siamese. And you? What are you?'

'Me? I'm alternative and colourful. And ugly,' I say.

'Hey, you're a funny kid, Frankie von Rubbish-Heap-Mountain. I like you.'

'So what's it like being a breed?' I ask. I do genuinely want to know. And I think I might be a bit jealous.

'Lonely,' she replies.

'Lonely?'

'I only ever meet Siamese cats. And even then only sometimes. My humans have forbidden me to mix with anyone else.'

'Are they racists?'

'Of course they're racists. But they call themselves breeders.'

'Breeders. Wow.'

And that's how I met the famous Bianca von Hosenwalde-Wolfenstein. Pure Siamese. You've probably heard of her: she used to be *the* big name in Hollywood.

'But then some young thing came along, a Maine Coon . . . three wiggles of her fluffy little arse and I was out on mine. Cast aside. That's how it works here, kid. It's dog-eat-dog. But trust me, you're lucky to have met me. Good ol' Bianca will see you right.'

I'm grateful for the help, because I haven't a clue what you're meant to do at a casting audition.

'Listen, kid, I'm going to give you a few tips. I'll even tell you the juicy little secret to stardom. That way you'll go all the way to the top. Wanna know the secret?'

I nod.

'Well, of course you do. But look, first you gotta do an old lady a little favour. See the dog at the back there, in the corner?'

And sure enough, there's a dog I didn't notice lurking in the shadows. Near the door that brought me to Second Level Down.

'Go over to him and tell him you need some of the good stuff for good ol' Bianca. Can you do that for me, sweetheart?'

I nod.

'What kind of dog is he?'

'A Deerhound.'

'Does he have a name too?'

'Dealer.'

'Dealer? That's his name?'

'Exactly. Now hurry along, Frankie!'

12. Bro

I cross the hall, thinking everything will be *just grand* once I've learnt the secret to Hollywood stardom. *Your luck's in, Frankie!*

There's just one problem. Dealer the Deerhound seems to be growing bigger and bigger the closer I get to him. And by the time I reach him, he's three or six times bigger than me. My legs suddenly start shaking, and when I greet him my voice goes all high-pitched and squeaky.

'Hey, Deerhound. How's it going? I was just . . .'

'Hey bro, speak up, man.'

'I was just after . . . some Good Stuff. For my friend Bianca.' Dealer looks down at me. He says nothing at first and just licks his bottom. I wait patiently.

I don't know if you've ever crossed paths with a Deerhound before, but this one is basically a towering mass of dark hair. I can hardly see Dealer's eyes through the curtain that hangs down over his face. He has a sort of centre parting and a pointy muzzle poking through it.

'How much, bro?' Dealer asks.

'I'm Frankie. Not *Bro*,' I say, thinking it would be good to point this out.

'OK, Frankie bro. So how much?'

'How much what?' I say.

'Of the good stuff, bro.'

And now I'm presented with a new dilemma. *How much?* I don't even know what I'm asking for! I mean, what is *the Good Stuff* anyway?

'One . . . portion?'

'OK, bro. What you got for me?' asks Dealer.

'Me? Nothing. I was just sent to collect it.'

'Oh, I see. So you want my good stuff without giving me anything in return? Is that how it is?'

Dealer's voice sounds threatening now.

'What am I supposed to give you?'

'A chew bone with chicken. That's my going rate. I also accept a chew stick with chicken. Or a rabbit neck. But give nothing, get nothing. So how about it, bro?'

I shake my head. Then Dealer thrusts his pointy muzzle right up close to my ear and whispers: 'If you've got nothing for me, then I've. Got nothing. For you. Now piss off!'

To be honest, I don't know what makes me stand my ground. I'm visibly scared. But I'm also in the depths of despair, and in my sudden desperation, I summon up all my courage to tell Dealer that I'm afraid I can't piss off. Not without the Good Stuff. Because I need it urgently in order to learn the secret to stardom.

Before I know it, I'm telling him about Pussica Purrilenko, how I wrote her a poem in the moonlight and languished in front of her window for an age, speechless with desire, and that stardom and Hollywood are my only chances of conquering her heart. Perhaps he too has been in love before, I add, and knows how it feels when your heart's breaking and there are days when you're so lovesick you just want to lie under an old bathtub softly whimpering and life is as dark as a forest in the night.

Suddenly I hear a sniff above my head, and look up to see a big, glistening tear hanging off the end of Dealer's long muzzle. It's the most enormous tear I've ever seen, as big as a raspberry, which is sort of logical really, because huge dogs *would* cry huge tears. As it turns out, Deerhounds are highly sensitive sorts, personality-wise. By now, Dealer's face fur is soaked with raspberry-sized tears, and he tells me between sniffs that mine is the dumbest and most moving story he's ever heard.

'Really?' I reply in amazement.

And he says: 'I'm *overcome*, bro. So emotional. Wow! I haven't cried this much since *Titanic*.'

Dealer tells me he was once madly in love. Sadly, it never worked out. Religious differences. I think it best not to pry any further, as Dealer has already done enough blubbing.

'And you really don't know what the Good Stuff is?'

'Not the foggiest, Dealer.'

'There's a lot you don't know, bro.'

'I know. I'm a country cat.'

Dealer raises his back end, and just as I think he's going to start the whole licking routine again, he raises it some more, and I see that he's hidden some small, transparent bags under his hairy coat. He pushes one of them towards me with his paw.

'That's the Good Stuff?'

It looks like dried grass.

'Catnip. Premium quality,' says Dealer.

I've heard of catnip before, and that it drives cats wild.

'But I can't give you anything for it.'

'Look, Frankie. Truth is, I haven't bawled like that in ages. And that's payment enough. Did me a world of good, bro. My breed are lifelong melancholics, you know. Can't be cured, but a cry helps. Now do me a favour and piss off, please.'

Bewildered, I saunter off with the bag in my mouth, feeling like a big cat returning triumphant from a hunt. Frankie Lionheart! Naturally, I'm itching to tell Bianca the whole story of my adventure with Dealer, but she isn't even listening. 'Cut the crap, kid, and gimme the Good Stuff. Hand it over!'

She tears the bag open greedily with her claws. Takes a deep sniff. Sticks her nose right in. Her eyes widen and within seconds, she's rolling around wildly in the catnip. Over and over again. It's . . . bizarre.

'Hello? *Hello?*' I try to attract her attention. 'Bianca? You were going to tell me the secret to stardom? Remember?'

She stops rolling for a moment and looks at me. Her blue eyes are cold and hard. 'The secret to stardom? OK. Here's the big secret kid: never trust a strange cat in Hollywood. Now beat it, you cretinous dimwit! Go on, get lost!'

I trudge back through the hall, bewildered, disappointed and sick to my stomach. Finally I collapse in a corner.

The worst part wasn't the deception itself. The worst part was that Bianca was absolutely right. I *was* a cretinous dimwit. Someone who would probably believe anything if it sounded good. And when you feel like a cretinous dimwit, all you want to do is run away or jump into a deep hole in the woods. And that's just what I wanted to do at that moment: go back to my village, where I belonged. Back to my good friends, even if some of them only have three legs. No more castles in the air. After all, they're hardly going to be looking for cretinous dimwits here in Hollywood. Or putting up a sign saying: 'Who wants to be a movie star? Cretinous dimwits welcome!'

The only problem is, in my eagerness to visit Dealer, I had lost Gold in the crowd. There was no sign of him. And another problem is that I'm so ravenous my legs have started to turn to jelly. And yet *another* problem is that all the other problems are driving me ever deeper into despair. That's often the way it goes with problems, unfortunately. Once you've got one, you've got another, and it all spirals from there. I guess that's life.

So I go back to the desk where the woman with the red claws and the man with the furless head were sitting earlier, plonk myself down and wait for Gold, thinking: *do the smart thing for once, Frankie.* And the smart thing is to wait in the place where you last saw the missing person. But Gold doesn't turn up. And soon I'm not just starving, but thirsty too. I'm at my wits' end, and the whole waiting game no longer seems so smart after all, because you just sit there on your backside going crazy. But then I notice something: next to the desk is a big door, and cats are going through it with their humans and coming out again a little while later. The humans are saying to the cats: 'That went really well, Jacqueline!' Or: 'Why were you so agitated, Peter?' Or: 'You could at least have pretended to like it, Lucy!' I observe these comings and goings for a while, looking and listening. And when the next person comes out, leaving the door open for a moment, I quickly sneak in.

It turns out there's a room behind the door. Sitting in it are several humans, including Red Claws and Furless Head. And there are these little suns on sticks. They give off such a bright light that it makes your eyes sting. But I can't see Gold anywhere.

I'm just about to sneak out again when I suddenly get a whiff of something. A real noseful. And then I see something. You'll never believe it, my friends! At first, I suspect it to be another of those mean Hollywood tricks. Because even if I am a cretinous dimwit, I do know there are some things that simply don't happen in this life. Like a fat juicy mouse sticking its head right into my mouth, offering itself up and saying: '*Bon appétit*, Frankie dear.'

Or a pack of wolves dropping by to say, 'We think you're super-smart and attractive, Frankie the Greatest. In fact, we're so impressed with you, we want you to be our Head Wolf from now on.'

Or me walking through the woods and finding the

Professor's fourth leg, and us glueing it back in place with spit, and it staying on!

None of that stuff is real though.

What I see and smell in Hollywood right now, however, is absolutely real. There it is: a bowl of food, just sitting there as if it's fallen from the heavens. Someone has even put a vegetable garnish on top. They needn't have bothered on my account, though it does look pretty.

I inch my way towards it, low to the ground, so the humans won't notice. I'm so hungry, I wolf the lot. The only thing that puts me off my stride a bit are the suns, which are shining directly on the bowl. And look, if you're thinking: *really funny story, Frankie*, then just wait till you hear the rest. Because suddenly, the humans all spring into action, saying things like: 'Jane, which cat is that? Check the list, please, will you?' And 'Tom, did you get that? Are we rolling? Get me a close-up!' And 'Wow. This one just rocks up and gets stuck in! As if it actually liked the stuff.' And 'Look at this cat scoffing!' And 'It's super-*authentic*, don't you think?' And: 'Yes, that pose is so *authentic*!' This seems to be their favourite word.

Then this human comes up to me carrying a big box on his shoulder. So I hiss at him, and I hold nothing back. I can't bear being disturbed when I'm eating, you see. It's just bad manners. And when I've finished I lick my chops, as you do, to catch the last bits of sauce.

'Did you see that? OMG! This one's really playing to the camera! Have you found its name on the list yet, Jane?'

And so it goes on. Until I hear a familiar voice behind me.

'Frankie! There you are, dammit. I've been looking for you all over the place!'

I'm mightily glad Gold has found me. Though I have to empty the bowl first. Meanwhile, the humans in the room rush up to Gold and start talking to him excitedly. With paw-shakes and meaningful nods of the head . . . the whole shebang. Eventually, Gold comes up to me.

'What have you been up to, Frankie?' he asks.

'Me? Nothing. Just eating. I was hungry.'

'The film guys are beside themselves.'

'Because of me?'

'Yes, of course.'

'Wait till they see me in the audition. I can do all sorts! Jumping, darting, chasing, hissing, lurking, watching, waiting, stalking . . .'

'Frankie. That *was* the audition.'

'Huh? I don't get it.'

'You're top of their list. Congratulations!'

'What?'

'Yep, Frankie! Looks like you're going to be the new face of Sauce Supreme. Who'd have thought?'

'Huh?'

Even long after we'd got into the car and left the city with its towers and zebra buildings behind us, I'm still left scratching my head. Because the whole thing was just so bizarre. I'd love to have chatted to Flipper sometime about his casting experiences. But I guess that's just Hollywood for you, my friends. You can have grand ambitions and you can chase after your dreams till you're blue in the face. But you could also just sit around, fill your boots and become famous. Because if I've learnt anything, it's that Hollywood is a place for people who do nothing. You just have to do nothing *authentically*. That's my secret to stardom for you.

We drive back through the big wide world again. Along an endless road, past fields and meadows and woods. I creep on to Gold's lap and he strokes my head while the car roars and shakes like mad. But it doesn't scare me any more. And as we're driving along together like that, Gold and me, I feel really happy. I don't think I've ever felt so happy in my life. I want that moment to last for ever.

13. Planets

The air smelt different. And the first to notice it was Muscles Nutkin, as we sat that evening on Rubbish Heap Mountain, gazing into the twilight.

'Smell that, Frankie? Autumn's on its way,' he says.

I open the holes in my nose wide, and sure enough, there's an autumnal nip in the air, a hint of coolness and damp earth.

'Ah, quality air!' says Muscles Nutkin, breathing deeply. 'You won't get air like this in Hollywood.'

'Air is air,' I reply flatly.

'No, Frankie. No. Air like this, with all these fabulous smells, you can only get that here. Believe me.'

This has been going on for days. Ever since I told my friends about Hollywood, Muscles Nutkin has been in a funny mood and keeps saying things like: 'Look at the clear water in this puddle: you won't find water like that in Hollywood, my friend!'

Or: 'Hear the wind rustling in the trees, Frankie? Such a fabulous sound. You won't hear that in Hollywood, I can tell you.' Or: 'Just look at this big fat yellow corn kernel! Surely you don't believe they have those in Hollywood? Surely not, Frankie?'

'Hey, I'm not going away,' I say, laying a paw on Muscles' brawny little shoulder. And we sit quietly like that for a while on the mountain, watching the night fall from the sky.

'Are you quite certain you're not going away?'

'Well, maybe briefly,' I say. 'To make a film. Or when I'm meeting famous people in Hollywood, to talk about important things over lunch.'

'What important things?'

'No idea. World peace, perhaps. That sort of thing.'

'Do you know much about world peace then, Frankie?'

'Not yet. But how hard can it be? At the end of the day, world peace is just like any other peace.'

'That's very wise, Frankie.'

'D'you think so?'

'It sounds wise to me.'

'Perhaps you can come with me to Hollywood sometime. We'll all go together: you, the Professor, Gold and me.'

'Gold too?'

'He has the car.'

'True.'

'And he can drive it.'

'True. There is that.'

'Besides, Gold's really not so bad. He might not be able to show it, but he's actually pretty decent for a human.'

Soon the moon appears and the stars above us start to multiply. It's a glorious sight. The sky is a glittering, glowing dome, and for a moment, I feel like we're invincible. Like we'll live for ever. Though I can't explain why looking up at the stars brings that feeling out in me.

'How come the moon's yellow, by the way? Do you know, by any chance, Frankie?'

'I guess they built it like that.'

'But sometimes it's not as yellow as that.'

'Yeah, sometimes it's a bit pale.'

'Weird how it just hangs there, isn't it?'

'Totally weird. But totally awesome too.'

'Yeah, totally awesome. It's quite something, the moon. Even when it's only half a moon. D'you reckon they can see us?'

'Who?'

'The moon dwellers.'

'Of course. If we can see the moon from here, they can see us. Stands to reason.'

'Let's give them a wave, then.'

And we wave at the moon until our paws ache.

'Do you know the Planet of the Apes?' I ask.

'No. What's a *planet*?'

'A planet's a star. Like the ones up there. I saw it on TV once. Fascinating. Somewhere up there is a star where the apes are in charge. They ride around on horses and rule over everyone. Even humans.'

'No way!' Muscles Nutkin gawps at me.

'It's true! I saw it on TV. There's definitely a Planet of the Apes up there somewhere. No kidding.'

'D'you think the moon could be the Planet of the Apes?'

'Maybe. We'd have to ask an ape. Do you know any apes?'

'Nah. You?'

'Nah.'

'D'you know what would be really amazing, Frankie? If there was a Planet of the Squirrels up there. Just imagine! Squirrels and nut trees and nut bushes and nut flowers everywhere. Everything made of nuts. And the squirrels would ride around on horses and make the rules.'

'Yes, that would be amazing. And I'd be on the planet opposite – the Planet of the Cats – and we could visit each other.'

'Exactly! But . . . how would we visit each other?'

'We'd ride over on the horses. There are bridges between the stars, and you can ride over them.'

'Of course, Frankie. Now you say it, I can't believe I hadn't figured it out myself.'

'But d'you know what would be even better? The Planet of the Cool Animals. Only animals you can get along with would live there. Like you, me, the Professor and a few others we get to choose. No arseholes like raccoons and their ilk.'

'And no eagles to hunt me.'

'And no swans, magpies or wolves.'

'And no martens, weasels or owls.'

'And no migratory birds.'

'And no humans.'

'No humans?'

'No one needs humans, if you ask me, Frankie.'

'Hmm . . . but humans are smart. And they're good workers. Someone would have to build the bridges between the planets for us. And feed the horses. And do all the other stuff we don't want to do.'

'OK, perhaps we'll take a few humans with us. Man, I wish I could ride there with you right now. The Planet of the Cool Animals. Amazing.'

'Shhh! Quiet!'

'What's up?'

'Did you hear that?'

There's a rustling noise coming from somewhere. The snap of a twig.

'There's someone there,' I say.

'Yes. But who?'

'How should I know? Keep quiet!'

We peer out into the dark, ears pricked. More rustling. And snuffling.

'We'd better get out of here, Frankie.'

'Shhh!'

A shadow is creeping through the rubbish. It's coming straight towards us. And then I smell that familiar smell.

'Shit. Speak of the devil. A raccoon,' I whisper.

Muscles Nutkin shoots off in a flash, shimmying up a birch tree.

'Frankie, there! I can see him! Watch out! There he is!' he calls down. And I'm sure he means well and all that. But even a raccoon with a hearing impediment would have discovered us by now.

The raccoon comes meandering towards me with his poncy raccoon walk. Raccoons always look so ridiculous walking like that. This one is bigger and stronger than me. A great lump of a raccoon. And to be honest, the smart thing would have been to leg it at this point.

No question. But there are times when a tomcat just can't do that. The rubbish heap is my home, you see. It's *my* rubbish heap. Old Mrs Berkowitz never understood that. When I came to her with bloody ears, she would shake her head, crying, 'Oh Frankie, you silly boy! Why do you always have to get into a fight?'

The answer is, it's just in my nature. Can't help it. I'm a *territorial animal*, and sometimes, a cat's just gotta do what a cat's gotta do. And thinking about it, it's a wonder humans don't get that. Because all my experience of humans so far tells me they're territorial animals too.

Then Muscles Nutkin calls down from the birch tree again: 'I'm going to get help, Frankie!', and tears off.

The raccoon opens his mouth wide, hissing and spitting. I see his sharp teeth in the moonlight. You wouldn't believe those cute raccoon faces could conceal such beastly sharp teeth. I mean, with some animals you can tell right away. If you meet a wolf, for example, and he grins and says *hello*, you can be pretty certain he's about to bite your head off. But with a raccoon, it's different. At first, everyone thinks they're cute, but it would be a mistake to underestimate them. I made that mistake myself once and lost half an ear. I was only a kitten then and knew nothing. I was on my way through the village one night when I came across these two raccoons. So I stopped to have a chat with them, because I was a bit lonely and thought they looked like friendly sorts. But they really beat the shit out of me. One of them took a bite out of my ear, and when he realized what he had in his mouth, and that it was too chewy to eat, he spat it out again. And my half an ear went flying through the air in a great arc. I never saw it again, though I still dream about it sometimes.

This time, when the fat lump of a raccoon opens his mouth, I go straight for him. I'm using the element of surprise, you see. I land him one good and proper with my claws. And another. I'm quick off the mark, and he's clumsy on account of being so fat. I don't pull my punches. The raccoon just looks baffled and hisses at me. Racoons are utterly fearless, I'll give them that. They can take a beating, and you've got to respect them for that.

And then suddenly, he clears off. He's not scared but he seems to have lost interest, as if he's thinking: *sod it, I can't be doing with this.* But that's when I make my mistake. Now that it's clear he's going to leave me alone, that I have emerged triumphant, I get cocky. Like I sometimes do in a scrap, when I feel like I'm winning. I call the mistake 'Opening My Big Mouth'. So I fling a few choice insults after him. Call him a cretin, that sort of thing. The raccoon turns, looks at me for a moment, then comes for me, all guns blazing.

He whacks me on the head and all over with his hellish claws. I see a flash in my left eye and let out a terrible yowl. It's like someone's suddenly switched off the light. Another massive blow hits me in the face and my knees give way. I topple over sideways, blood streaming from my muzzle. The raccoon's on top of me now; I can smell his revolting breath. He bites me in the side. He bites me in the back of the neck. He buries his sharp teeth into my flesh. It's nothing like in the films I've seen where humans fight each other. When one of them begs for mercy, the other lets him go. Not a chance: the raccoon drags me through the dirt and carries on walloping me. *This is it, Frankie*, I think to myself. *You're a goner.* Just time to give thanks to the Supreme Commander (or whoever) for my life. It's been a blast.

Looking back, I reckon I've been really lucky. I've slept a lot, and a few people have even loved me. That's a good deal of luck, if you ask me. Only now it's all over, the luck's running out.

Then, out of my one eye, I see a dishevelled dressing gown – and the man in it – rushing headlong towards me. Leading the charge is Muscles Nutkin, shouting, 'Frankie! We're coming for you! Are you still alive? Frankie!'

It's quite a scene: Gold puffing and panting in his pathetic dressing gown, Muscles Nutkin shimmying up the birch tree again, me half dead on the ground and, in the midst of it all, the raccoon. But what happens next takes the biscuit. Gold lets out an almighty yell I've never heard the likes of. No animal I know can yell like that, so full of rage and despair. He charges towards the raccoon with a full battle cry, pelting him with whatever he can grab: stones, bits of rubbish . . . Objects are flying around all over the place. The raccoon's going berserk, but Gold seems undaunted. Here is a man who knows no fear. He's kicking and lashing out without a hint of hesitation. I feel a wave of pride well up inside me. And a little fear too, to be honest. Gold seems past the point of no return. He's like a madman. Even madder than the raccoon. Finally, the raccoon runs away, but Gold carries on yelling for some time. Until I murmur weakly, 'That's enough now. It's all right. I'm all right.'

Gold carries me down the mountain, holding me close to his chest like a baby. I see the lovely moon. Somewhere up there is the Planet of the Cool Animals, and I vow to go there sometime before I die.

14. Morons

Everything hurt. Everything burned. I was completely shattered, and I could hardly see anything out of my left eye. Gold had laid me down on the couch in the Deserted House and fetched a blanket to keep me warm. Then he sat by the phone talking to Anna Komarova, who he now called Anna. And Muscles Nutkin and the Professor were there too.

They were all gathered round me like a family – though I must say I can't think of any other family consisting of a human, a tomcat, a squirrel and a three-legged dachshund. And they were all anxious to know if I needed anything, if I was comfortable, if I was *sure* I was comfortable. And Muscles Nutkin kept asking, 'Frankie, how are you?' And I would say 'OK'. And then a moment later he would ask again: 'And how are you *now*, Frankie?' It got on my nerves a little, if I'm being honest. But it was oddly wonderful too. I can't remember the last time anyone had cared that much about me. And it almost seemed a shame that it was happening now, when I was so far gone. Otherwise I'd have had more chance to enjoy it.

'Man, I'm so glad you're still alive,' says Muscles Nutkin. 'That was a close shave, Frankie.'

'I thought you were never coming back,' I say in a wobbly voice.

'Man, I dashed straight back to the Deserted House to fetch Gold as soon as you went for the raccoon. But he was . . . busy.'

'Busy?'

'Um . . . with the string here.'

Muscles Nutkin points to the ceiling. And there it is again: the ginormous piece of string. I'd been too far gone to notice it.

'I sat at the window and shouted like mad,' Nutkin explained. 'But Gold didn't respond. He was standing on the chair with the string around his neck. Practically dangling from it, he was. Like a nut from a tree.'

'Perhaps he didn't hear you?'

'Of course he heard me!'

'What did you shout?'

'*Help! Frankie!* That's all the Humanish I know. But he definitely understood it. He looked at me as he dangled there. He should have come straightaway, Frankie.'

'Yes, he really should have come straightaway. But he does like playing with that string. Mad about it, he is.'

'I still don't think it was right to take his time like that though. After all, it was literally a matter of life and death.'

'No, it wasn't right.'

'What do *you* think, Professor?' Muscles Nutkin asks. 'Don't you agree it was bad of Gold to go on playing with his string before coming to help Frankie?'

The Professor doesn't say a word, but just stares at the string like it's some great miracle.

'Hey, Prof, what's up?'

He shakes his grey head gently. Then he says in his hoarse whisper: 'Morons. You absolute morons.'

I guess I don't need to tell you what the Professor – who's the smartest animal on the planet – went on to explain to us. About the string and all that. You can imagine. Because *you're* not a moron. Or at least I hope you're not. And I'm sure you can also imagine how stupid I felt. I'm a prize idiot. All the time I've been telling you this story, and the penny never dropped!

Well, now it has: I get it. At least, the thing itself. *Suicide*. Only I couldn't believe it. Because there's a difference between understanding and believing. And even if I were the smartest tomcat under the sun, I would never have believed that Gold wanted to die.

And yet, everything else I can believe. I believe the worst shit. Did I ever tell you how I was born? I slipped out of my mother the way all cats do. Together with Number 1, Number 2, Number 3, Number 4, Number 6 and Number 8. My siblings. All soft and weak and no bigger than a human's hand. Soon after, the human whose farm we lived on put my family in a sack. And he stuffed the sack, with its wriggling and mewling contents, into the depths of a water barrel until there was no more wriggling and no more mewling. As I hid behind a stack of timber, the human cursed under his breath. 'Jesus Christ! Always the same shit.'

I had no trouble believing what evil a human was capable of in that moment, that this man would be capable of murder. But that a human could do that to himself – *that* I couldn't believe.

Gold puts the phone down. 'She'll be here right away, Frankie,' he says, gently. 'How are you, pal?'

I could have burst into tears. I watch him as he climbs on to the chair that's still in place under the string, takes the string down, winds it up and puts it under the couch. I hear a small car driving up the Big Road, and moments later the door flies open and Anna Komarova appears in the room. She takes one look at us all gathered there, three animals and one human.

'Bloody hell!' she says, dropping her briefcase.

15. A Pair of Losers

When I wake up, it's still dark, and there's something around my neck. A big, mysterious thing. I paw away at it, but the thing won't let go of my neck and I grow panicky and unsettled. I paw away at myself, until suddenly I remember what the thing is. *A protective collar.*

That's what Anna Komarova called it. She said other things too, of course, like '*Dear, oh dear,* my little Pooshock.' I was in such a state she positively winced. My left eye was particularly bad. She told Gold I might be 'visually compromised', but I wasn't interested in compromises. I just wanted to be able to see again. She dripped something into my eye, shoved something up my front and rear end, and finally stuck the Big Mysterious Thing over my head to stop me scratching around my eye.

It was driving me. Round. The. Bend.

I jump down off the sofa, listening and looking. The house is completely silent, as if there's no one else home, which makes me uneasy. *Where's Gold?* I peer under the sofa: the string is still there. I creep through the house, having to make an extra effort not to crash into everything because I only have one eye left and the Big Mysterious Thing stretches right past my ears. I look everywhere. Finally, I drag myself up the stairs. It's only a short staircase, but it feels never-ending. I really am on my last legs. I creep into Gold's room to find him lying there on his back, asleep, his muzzle wide open.

I watch him for a while. Most humans look utterly ridiculous when they're asleep. Much more so than any animal I know.

But baby humans – they don't look ridiculous. There's something undeniably cute about them, like cats. I once saw a baby human asleep with my own eyes. Don't ask me where. But I licked its head. I remember that. It was just sleeping so sweetly, I couldn't help myself.

I jump into the bed next to Gold and watch him a while longer. Then I poke him on the nose. I can't wait for ever.

'Gold, wake up. I need to talk to you. It's important.'

'Frankie? What . . . What's up . . . ? It's the middle of the night.'

'I know. Listen. You mustn't die.'

'Frankie . . .'

'Listen to me! Dying's a really bad idea. I mean, I could maybe understand it if you were an earthworm. An earthworm has no arms, no legs, no head. It's just a worm. That's no life, if you ask me. But I know a few earthworms, and even they never think of doing themselves in. And they're just worms! But you're a human. You have so much to live for. You can do anything! And you have this house here, and you have me, and you . . .'

'Frankie, stop it.'

'No, I won't stop it! I don't want you to end yourself.'

'What am I supposed to say? Sorry? Won't happen

again? It just doesn't work like that, Frankie. It's not that easy.'

'Yes it is! Living is easy. Any fool can live.'

'I'm trying, Frankie. I really am.'

'Then try harder!'

I settle down next to Gold, right in the crook of his arm, my paws pressed up against his warm body. And there we lie.

Two losers. Side by side in the early-morning light.

'Why can't you just be a little bit happy? Like other humans?'

'Because there's only one thing that would make me happy, Frankie. All I want is to have Linda back again. And that's never going to happen. Trust me, I really thought I could do it. I thought I'd get over this one day and live a normal life again. But I'm a self-pitying, self-loathing, depressed mess. *That's* the truth. Not a day goes by where I don't feel angry, despairing, lonely, ashamed. I don't feel joy any more. These days, a good day is just one when I don't want to kill myself.'

'That's barmy.'

'No, it's an illness. I'm sick, Frankie.'

'Then go to the doctor. Go to Anna Komarova. She'll stick something up your front and rear end and you'll feel better again in no time!'

'I wish.'

'What kind of disease is it anyway?'

'The Everything-Is-Meaningless disease.'

'Never heard of it. But why meaningless? You've got me! I'm your Purpose in Life now, Gold.'

'You?'

'Of course. I promise you, I've got this. I mean, I must bring you some happiness, just by being around and all that? You get to stroke my silky-smooth fur, you enjoy having me near, and we have interesting conversations, don't we? And then you go shopping for me. You clean my toilet. Plus all the other little chores. Man, I gotta be honest with you, Gold, I'd be pretty glad to have a Purpose in Life like me!'

'But you don't need me, Frankie.'

'I have two friends. But the Professor's very old, and I worry he won't last much longer. And Muscles Nutkin is just a squirrel. He's so small, a fox snack just waiting to be eaten. Or struck dead. Or run over. And just like that, I'll be left all on my own . . . At least with you, I thought I was safe. Someone for forever.'

'Sorry, Frankie.'

'Perhaps you could just wait a bit.'

'What for?'

'Until *I'm* dead. Humans live longer than cats. And after I'm dead, you can still do yourself in. If you like.'

'I don't know if I can hang on that long, Frankie.'

'It's all me, me, me with you! What about yours truly?'

'Sorry you ended up with me, of all people. You deserved better.'

I can't fault his logic there. But the trouble is, I don't *want* better. Isn't that the whole problem when you're fond of someone? You want what you have right in front of you. You're not looking for 'better'.

'That's a fine lampshade Anna's hung round your neck,' says Gold, tapping my collar.

'And what if I became depressing too? Like you?'

'You mean depressed,' Gold replies.

'Yes, depressed. Whatever. Would it help you if we were the same? I wouldn't mind, you know. I'm already an agnostic. And a hedonist. I might as well be a depressivist as well.'

'You mean a depressive.'

'Sure. But how about it, seriously? Don't you think it's a great idea? Two depressives together – think of the fun we could have!'

I sit up and look at Gold. With my saddest, most melancholic face, and the Big Mysterious Thing that looks like a lampshade flapping round my head. Suddenly, Gold starts laughing. I'm so startled I nearly fall out of bed. It's the first time I've heard Gold laugh. To be honest, I didn't even know he could. But now that he's started, he can't seem to stop.

Eventually, he collects himself. 'Ah, thank you, Frankie,' he chuckles. 'I needed that.'

Honestly! Humans! You can't make heads nor tails of them.

Gradually, the sun comes up. Gold strokes my tummy, and I grow drowsier and drowsier. But I don't want the night to end.

Gold turns to me. 'If I die, Frankie, what would you miss? Nothing, surely?'

'What would I miss? A whole bunch of things. I'd miss sauce, for a start.'

'Sauce?'

'I was chewing on a sparrow the other day. But it was hard going. Too dry. The stuff you get from the Pet Shop is much better. More sauce. Sauce takes life to a whole new level.'

'You don't want me to die because you like sauce?'

'Now don't get offended. I'm just saying that sauce . . .'

'I'm not offended.'

'Do you like sauce?'

'Absolutely.'

'What's your favourite?'

'Couldn't say. There are so many good ones. Horseradish. Dill. Mustard. Tomato. Hard to choose.'

'My thoughts exactly. I'd like to have worked my way through all the best sauces before I die.'

'I had a parmigiana with Linda once. In Italy, ages ago. We were walking on some mountain or other, I can never remember the names of mountains. Anyway . . .'

'Where's Italy?'

'In the south.'

'Ah.'

'Anyway: parmigiana is a dish made from aubergines. With garlic and tons of basil, Parmesan, mozzarella, tomato purée. You put the whole thing in the oven, and it just smells divine. But the best thing about a parmigiana is the way the tomatoes, herbs and cheese blend into this amazing sauce. We dipped white bread into it and were in heaven. Yep, that was probably the best sauce of my life . . .'

'Oh, man, sauce. You can't beat it.'

'Sometimes, when I think of Linda, that's the very

thing that comes to mind: eating that damned parmigiana sauce together. Isn't that weird? It's the little things you remember in the end.'

'That doesn't sound weird at all to me.'

'Well . . .'

'And that's precisely why you don't want to go doing yourself in, Gold. Think about it: the dead can't eat sauce.'

'Perhaps you should write that on my tombstone. *No sauce for the dead.* I like it. Would you do that for me Frankie, my little Purpose in Life?'

16. Everything Will Be Fine

Anna Komarova came nearly every day to check up on me. And I reckon she also came to see Gold. At least, that's the impression I got. They spent a lot of time chatting to each other, and Gold seemed less depressed when she was there. You could really see it. Or rather, I could only half see it because my eye was so kaput. But you know what I mean. At any rate, I was glad when Anna Komarova came to see us and I was sad when she got into her little car and drove off again along the Big Road.

When I was alone with Gold, I couldn't stop worrying that he might hurt himself. He ate, drank, slept, talked and watched TV normally enough. But what was going on in his head, and whether it was full of life-ending thoughts, I didn't know. And that freaked me out. Because at any moment, either nothing at all could happen, or the worst could happen. I was on edge.

To make matters worse, I still couldn't see anything out of my left eye, and I was beginning to worry I might be blighted with half-vision for ever. And then I'd be *Frankie One-Eye. Frankie the Misfit. Frankie the Dead-Eyed Monster.*

I was mightily depressed. Anna Komarova would stroke my fur and say, 'Don't worry. Everything will be fine, my little Pooshock.' But in my experience, humans have a bit too much of a habit of saying things like that. Plus, it's a pretty dumb thing to say because everyone knows everything *won't* be fine. That's not how life works. Some of it will be good, and some of it will be bad, and that's if you're lucky. And that's the whole trouble.

Muscles Nutkin often visited me. He would sit next to me on the couch drumming his paws on my lampshade because he said it made such 'a funky sound', and he even reckoned there were advantages to having only one eye.

'Think of the positives, Frankie.' Of course, he was trying to cheer me up. Everyone was always trying to cheer me up these days.

'Name me one,' I said.

'It means you can't squint. It'll be your trademark thing, like a scar or something.'

'You can still squint with one eye.'

'Can you? Oh well, perhaps there aren't any positives then. Fancy a nut?'

Man, was I depressed. I stopped going out. I just didn't want anyone to see me like that, limping along with one eye and the lampshade rattling around my neck.

There are magpies to worry about, for a start. They'd make mincemeat of me. Sitting there on their branch hurling insults, cracking rude jokes and cackling their heads off. And everyone else would think me weak and frail. *That Frankie's over the hill now*, they'd think. *He's had his day.* And then they'd take over my patch, *my* territory, and set themselves up as the new boss.

But eventually I did go out. Because there was no other way. I popped over to the Professor's and joined him and Muscles: just three friends lying in the garden under the laden pear tree, talking about how we could help Gold. It was clear as day that he needed it. Gold had rescued me from the raccoon, and I would rescue him from himself in return. It couldn't be that difficult, after all.

All we needed was a good rescue plan and the follow-through to execute it. If we just put our heads together for a bit, we'd be sure to come up with *something*. Especially between three of us. Three clever brains working as one. *Swarm intelligence*: that's what birds call it.

The Professor was by far the most learned and world-wise, of course.

Turning to us both, he said gently, 'You know, I read something once. In the newspaper. Did you know I can read, by the way? Listen: one thing we know is that Gold isn't the only depressed person in the world. There are actually quite a few.'

'How many is *quite a few*?' I ask.

'Five, maybe six?' Muscles Nutkin offers.

'Three hundred and fifty million,' says the Professor.

'Oh. Wow.' I pause for a moment, a little lost for words.

'Blimey,' adds Muscles Nutkin.

'Imagine a huge city where all the humans are depressed,' says the Professor. 'And then imagine another huge city, and another, and another, and another . . .'

So I try to imagine what *millions* might look like in my

head. A city, and another city, and on and on for what feels like eternity. I try to fathom a number that big, but the nearest I can get to is picturing a herd of wildebeest charging across the savannah. Wildebeest as far as the eye can see. And all these wildebeest are depressed too. Somehow, that helps me to visualize it all a little.

'And what if they're all heading our way?' asks Muscles Nutkin with a slight panic in his voice. 'All these depressed people? Like a plague? What if Gold is just patient zero?'

'Nonsense!' says the Professor.

'Or what if it's spreading? Before we know it, we'll have an outbreak of depression here too, you mark my words, Frankie! You're living with a depressive. If it's contagious . . .'

'Nonsense!' I shout.

Though, to be honest, in my heart of hearts, I'm not quite sure how it all works.

'How do millions of humans get depression if it's not contagious, Frankie? Hmm? Riddle me that,' whispers Muscles Nutkin pointedly.

And you have to admit, it's a fair question. One none of us seems to know the answer to.

'Does anyone know a depressive we could ask, perhaps?' I say.

'What about Owl?' suggests Muscles Nutkin. 'He always looks so miserable.'

'I think that's just because he's an owl?' I reply. 'That's not depression. His face just does that.'

Having ruled Owl out, we did some brainstorming

and came up with a few animals we knew with, let's say, *melancholic tendencies*. But the question remained, *were* they depressed? And did any of them actually want to end it all? We tried as hard as we could, but we couldn't think of any that did. Not a single one! Who knew? I guess we animals must be pretty cheerful on the whole.

After a whole lot of thinking, more than we were used to, we concluded that wanting to end yourself had to be an exclusively human disease. Which was another big mystery to us. I mean, it just *didn't make sense*. Why humans, of all people? When they're so wise and so powerful, and they can do all sorts of clever tricks and achieve such great things. Was it their diet? Their thinning, balding, pathetic fur? Was the weight of ruling the world getting to them? We didn't have the answers, shaking our heads in disbelief.

For what it's worth, here's what I think, dear humans. And let's keep this between you and me, OK? This might sound ridiculous, and please don't laugh, but could it be that you sleep too little and think too much? Because you see, my life is exactly the opposite: I spend nearly all day asleep. I wake up for a while and do a few bits and pieces here and there, and then I go back to sleeping and dreaming. The big advantage of this lifestyle is that you don't get to see too much of the world. Because if you see too much of the world and think too much . . . well, I don't know. Maybe it makes you sick and gives you a gloomier, darker outlook on life? But what do I know? I'm just a friendly neighbourhood tomcat.

The Professor, who – being a dog – is of course

devoutly religious, suggested that Gold pray every day to the Supreme Commander. Ideally as often as possible. *Pray* the depression away, he said. For his part, Muscles Nutkin suggested a nut diet and plenty of exercise, to help Gold *run* away from the depression. And I suggested trying to get him laughing again. Humans seem pretty happy when they're laughing. Like that one time when I heard Gold having a good old guffaw, one of those deep belly laughs. The answer came to me like a bolt of lightning.

'A clown! We need a clown!'

Muscles Nutkin and the Professor's eyes lit up. 'Great idea, Frankie!'

One *minor* flaw in our plan: no one knew any clowns, or where we might find one. Quickly realizing that my spark of genius was a non-starter, we moved on.

I won't bother telling you the other suggestions. They didn't really hit the mark either. We went on racking our brains and talking ourselves round in circles as we sat under the pear tree, waiting for inspiration to fall from above. But all that fell was the odd pear, it being autumn and all. I felt desperate. There can't be anything worse than seeing someone you care about go to the dogs and all you can do is watch from afar, helpless. It breaks you inside.

Can it be that I'm cursed? Not that I know much about curses, mind. I just couldn't shake the feeling that I must be Frankie the Damned. Nearly everyone in my life who meant anything to me has gone to the dogs. My siblings – Number 1, Number 2, Number 3, Number 4, Number 6 and Number 8. Old Mrs Berkowitz. And now Gold as well.

Sounds pretty much like a curse to me. And I don't know what you're supposed to do when you're cursed. Perhaps I should steer clear of all humans and all animals and live a solitary life deep in the forest. Or with other cursed creatures.

When another pear drops from the tree, the Professor pipes up.

'Frankie, my boy. I think you need to talk to this Anna Komarova about Gold.'

Truth be told, I'd had the same thought.

'But what about the *Three Golden Rules*, Professor? Rule One: act stupid. Rule Two: act stupid. Rule Three: act stupid?'

'True. But this is a real emergency. Talk to her. She's a doctor . . .'

'Yes, an animal doctor, not a human one!'

'But we can't do this on our own. We need all the help we can get, Frankie.'

'Yes, Frankie! Talk to her!' says Muscles Nutkin excitedly. 'But word of advice? Offer her a nut first, so she knows you come in peace.'

I trudge back along the Big Road. I know life can be good. But nothing was good at the moment, and I felt a deep darkness. I saw something on TV once where a human got into this crazy machine and travelled through time. Backwards into the past or forwards into the future, but always away from life as we know it. And oh how I wished I could do the same! But I didn't know anyone with a machine like that, any more than I knew any clowns. Sometimes it's not easy being a tomcat. Because if something's really depressing you and there's a darkness in your heart, you can't just run away. You have to grin and bear it.

'Hello, Frankie.'

I stop in my tracks, ears pricked, fur on end. I can't hear all that well because of the lampshade, but I know who it is instantly. Those damned magpies, directly overhead! Well, let me tell you, they might be up for taking the piss and ripping me to shreds, but I'm here to say, *not today, amigos. Not with me.*

'Clear off, you hooligans!' I bellow, full of rage. 'Or I'll get you! I swear I'll come and eat the lot of you up for breakfast. I'm Frankie! And I will come for you, mark my words!'

Silence.

I look up cautiously, to where the magpies sit among the branches of the lime tree. Except there's no one there. I peer cautiously to my right. No one. I turn round slowly and . . . holy shit! I take a step back and nearly trip over my own paws. It wasn't magpies after all! Instead, standing before me is Pussica Purrilenko, radiant as ever.

She looks at me in alarm. I look at her in alarm. And so we stand for a little while like this, while I search for the right words to make up for my outburst and try to remember the words of the poem I wrote specially for her. But no words come.

My mind draws a blank.

My heart bumm-bumms in my chest.

'I thought . . .' I say eventually.

'Yes?'

'I thought . . . Sorry. I thought . . . you were a magpie.' My first words to her: *I thought you were a magpie*. What a plonker.

Pussica Purrilenko tilts her head slightly, as we cats have a tendency to do when we're puzzled, or when we hear something very odd, or very stupid.

'What happened to you?' she asks.

'To me?'

Pussica Purrilenko was so beautiful in that moment, I'd quite forgotten that I wasn't exactly looking my best. Isn't that always just the way things go? You spend your life wishing someone would notice you, and when finally, by some miracle, they do, you have one eye, a terrible limp and a lampshade round your neck. Life is cruel and unfair.

'I . . . it was a raccoon . . .' I stammer. 'I . . . had a fight with a raccoon.'

'Really?'

'Yes.'

'You're very brave, Frankie.'

She actually knew my name. I didn't know how, nor did I care, as long as I could go on hearing it tumble from her pretty little muzzle.

And then she wanted to know all about it, the whole story. How I had fought with the raccoon, and then where, and why? So I tell her everything. Gradually I find the words, occasionally embellishing one or two details here and there. But I reckon that's OK when you're desperate to impress someone and only have one eye and a lampshade round your neck. A fox once explained to me that exaggerating isn't the same as lying. It's just telling the truth with a bit more colour and panache. I even tell Pussica Purrilenko about Hollywood, but funnily enough, she didn't seem particularly interested in all that, or the fact that I was practically a movie star now. Maybe she doesn't have a TV? And there we sat, side by side next to the Big Road, talking and gazing at the landscape that stretched out before us. And the whole time, I was itching to tell her how nice it was to be sitting here next to her, gazing at this view. And that what made me happy wasn't actually the view at all, which was rather ordinary. Deep in my chest I knew that there were other reasons this moment was so perfect. But I kept quiet in the end, because words . . . well, I don't know, sometimes they spoil everything.

'I live down there. In the red house,' she said as she was leaving. I nodded as if I didn't already know *exactly* where Pussica Purrilenko lived.

'Perhaps you'd like to pop by sometime?'

And then, just like that, she walked off down the Big Road, without stopping to turn around. I watched her go, my heart filled with longing. It would take me days to tell you everything that went through my head at that moment. Perhaps months, years! But suffice to say, it probably wouldn't be very interesting to you. These things are only interesting when you're in the thick of them and your emotions are surging through your belly.

Suddenly, I started running. Legged it as fast as I could, which, as you can imagine, wasn't very fast. I was determined to tell Gold everything: no one else, just him. Because I knew it would make him happy. I sprinted all the way to the Deserted House, with the lampshade banging and bobbing against my head. Man, did I run! I knew this might not be the trick that saves him or anything, but it would make him happy if I told him I'd taken a chance on love. I was convinced of it. And perhaps that would be a start, that little bit of happiness.

17. Into the Woods

When I finally reached the Deserted House, I found the front door locked shut. All the windows were locked too, which I thought was a bit odd. Peering through the big window into the house, I saw nothing. No one. I called Gold's name a few times too. Perhaps he was asleep. Perhaps he'd gone for a walk to the cemetery again, to talk to Linda. His old car was still outside the house as usual.

I settled down on the patio to wait, dreaming to myself. And even though most dreams are nonsense, I have to admit that I really enjoyed this one. First, I spoke to Anna Komarova, and then she spoke to Gold about the whole suicide thing. And in my dream, Gold suddenly came to his senses and was whistling tunes to himself again in no time. And guess what else? Pussica Purrilenko was there too, living with us! And Anna Komarova and her briefcase as well. In the evenings, we sat and watched animal documentaries together, which admittedly wasn't Gold's cup of tea, but he was outnumbered two animals and a vet to one, and didn't have a say. Fast-forward and Pussica Purrilenko turns to me one day and asks, 'Have you noticed anything, my darling Frankie?'

I would never be one to say anything, but she *had*

grown a bit plump. Too much Sauce Supreme methinks. But no! There were six or more little Frankies and Pussicas on the way! And there was no one around to throw them in a water barrel when they were born either. Gold gave them all the family name: Frankie 1, Frankie 2, Frankie 3, Frankie 4, and so on. At this point I was so excited by the prospect that I woke up, and alas, the dream vanished. I tried to find all the threads back again and carry on dreaming, but it was no use. Man, it's a pain when you lose a good dream like that, isn't it? Like you've been robbed.

I waited for Gold till dusk, and then I waited some more, well into the dead of night. I ate a few grasshoppers to keep the wolf from the door, then lay in the bushes and waited until the sun rose again over the lake. I waited the whole of the next day too. Unwelcome as the thought was, I began to wonder if something had happened. Something terrible.

I rejoined my friends, and we spent another whole day looking for Gold, just in case he was dangling from a string somewhere. We asked all the animals we knew, and we knew a lot. We spread the word, but no one had seen him. The day after that, I went into the woods and looked up at the trees. I went down to the river, but all I could hear was the gentle babbling of the water in the brook.

I went to Owl, who was perched on his branch, as usual.

'Hey, Owl, have you seen a human recently?' I ask him, my eyes sad and my whiskers drooping.

'Why, are you looking for one?'

'Yes. *My* human.'

'No one's been past here, I'm afraid.'

'Will you tell me if you see one?'

'Will do, Frankie.'

'Thanks. You're a good egg, Owl. Even if you do have a miserable face. I know it's not your fault.'

I searched and searched. And my friends searched and searched too. But all in vain. No one could find him. Gone without a trace.

I went back to waiting outside the Deserted House. I just lay there on the wooden bench by the door, with no desire to do anything except go on lying there, undisturbed by the world. Deep down, I knew what had happened, of course. But I couldn't bring myself to say it out loud. Not to anyone, not even to myself. I just whispered it, on the day the robin sang such a sad and beautiful song.

It sounded like a requiem.

The days passed, and eventually the Professor came along and asked whether he should fetch a fox to read the eulogy. I think Gold would have liked that – having a fox read a eulogy for him, embellished with all the flowery, poetic stuff only foxes know how to say about the dead – so I agreed. Perhaps it would have even made him laugh, up there in heaven. Or maybe it would give him a sense of his own significance. Humans like to feel significant. They tend to think their death is a huge loss to the world, but the truth is that life usually just goes on, unchanged. The world doesn't stop for you. It still looks just the same now as it always has. It looks the same as it did yesterday, and the same as it will tomorrow, and the day after tomorrow. A dark mood came over me thinking about it.

I didn't want a fox. I didn't want a eulogy. I lay curled up on the wooden bench in front of the house, head on my paws. It got dark, it got light: that was all. A swarm of bumblebees could have flown up my arse and I wouldn't have cared.

I think I must've been like that for quite a while, or even longer than a while. Muscles Nutkin reckoned I was depressed. But that didn't matter much to me now either.

18. Dear Frankie

I could hear a small car coming up the Big Road. A car door slammed, the garden gate creaked, and Anna Komarova ran towards me, briefcase in hand. I didn't budge, lying firmly in place on my bench. I didn't care to move any more. Besides, she was too late. Far, far too late.

When she was within a few tail lengths of me, Anna Komarova suddenly stood still. She stared at me with an odd look in her eyes, as if she thought I might bite.

'Hello, Frankie,' she said nervously, making sure to not come any closer. I could smell that she was scared. What on earth was this all about? And why did she call me *Frankie*? What had happened to *little Pooshock*?

She stood there for a while, watching me very closely, and then spoke quietly.

'I must be crazy to even ask this, but I'm going to all the same: do you understand what I'm saying, Frankie?'

And because she was so keen to know, and because I was past caring, I replied in Humanish.

'I do, yes.'

She let out a couple of shrill screams at first.

But I must say, it didn't last very long. She collected herself, and remained pretty calm, considering how freaked out she had been by my speaking Humanish. She is a vet after all, and she probably thought she knew all there was to know about animals.

'He told me you'd understand!' she cried. 'That crazy guy told me you would!'

Once she had calmed down a bit, Anna Komarova cautiously sat down next to me on the bench, fetching a piece of paper from her briefcase and holding it out to me.

'What's that?' I ask.

'A letter. For you, Frankie.'

'I can't read.'

'Shall I read it to you?'

'You tell me. What does it say?'

'It's from Richard.'

'Who's Richard?'

'Gold?'

My ears prick up.

'OK, I'll just read it to you for now, shall I? And then . . . never mind. I'll just read it to you. Ready?'

I nod and miaow all at once. No one's ever written me a letter before, after all. And this one's from a corpse, from beyond the grave. *Now* do you believe me when I say I'm cursed?

Dear Frankie,

If the people here knew that I'm writing you a letter, that I talk to a cat and that the cat talks to me, they would probably never let me out again. At least, not any time soon . . .

The fact is, I've been admitted into a loony bin. Anna can tell you what it's like and what I'm doing here. She brought me here. And I'm so sorry I just disappeared, Frankie. I had no choice. I reckon I'd have tried to end it all again otherwise. And you can't rescue me every time.

That I'm here at all is thanks to you (and Anna). I came to that house to die. And suddenly there you were at the window. You never asked me how I was. You never told me to pull myself together. You just yawned when I descended into self-pity. You simply had no idea. You were the most irritating, ignorant, wonderful distraction imaginable.

Sometimes when you were asleep and I was lying awake, I would bury my nose in your warm fur, and for a moment, I felt so comforted. Your smug snoring soothed me too. Yes, Frankie, you snore. Seeing you like that made me think: oh, to die and be reborn as a cat! In this facility, we're often told to think of a 'happy moment' and to hold on to it. I think of our trip to 'Hollywood'. That was the best day I've had in a long, long time. And I'm damned proud of you, my crazy Sauce Supreme Face. My little Purpose in Life.

You said: 'Living is easy. Any fool can do it.' But for me, it's an ordeal: getting up day after day, carrying on. I'm just so tired of it. I'm tired of my anger, my never-ending pain. I want to be light again, I want to get up one morning and see light ahead. I wish I was one of those fools who can simply live and enjoy it. Not just survive from one day to the next.

I don't know if I can do that.

You can stay in the house for now. Anna will take care of you – please be good to her. I hope we'll see each other again, Frankie.

I really do.

Your friend,
Gold
PS My bed is off limits!

Anna Komarova read me the letter over and over. Every time she got to the end, I pleaded with her to read it again.

Because let me tell you, there is no greater joy, and no better letter than one from a corpse who isn't dead. Believe me.

My mind was all over the place. On the one hand, I was incredibly glad that Gold was alive. In fact I was so happy I nearly bit my own tail. But I was also incredibly sad that he had gone away. And when your emotions are all mixed up like that, as I'm sure you know, the first thing to do is lick your privates, because you have to do *something*. And I'm sure I don't need to tell you twice that there's nothing like a good ol' lick to calm the nerves.

Then Anna Komarova told me about the loony bin – which she called a 'mental hospital' – and showed me a photo on her phone. In it was a big, old house in the woods, with a lake at the back.

Anna Komarova told me that the humans in the loony bin spend most of their time talking. They sit in a circle all day talking about their problems. Then there's someone called a *therapist* whose job it is to say things like, 'How does that make you feel, when you share your thoughts with the group?' And sometimes they all go running through the woods or paint pictures or make birds out of straw or lie on the ground and just breathe.

I don't know . . . I think I'd find it a little depressing, with all those depressives talking about how depressed they are. But I hope Gold isn't depressed any more. Or at least, that the people there can help him, and that the food's decent, with plenty of sauce, and that he's allowed to watch the fat men throwing arrows on late-night TV.

'So what do we do now?' I asked, after we'd been sitting there silently for a while, on the wooden bench in front of the house. Anna Komarova ran her hand through my fur.

'No idea, Frankie.'

'It's weird,' I said. 'How you can miss someone even though they've only just gone. Weird.'

'Yes, I miss him too.'

'D'you think he'll come back?'

'I hope so.'

'I think he'll come back. How's he going to manage without me? He can't get by in the world on his own.'

'True. You're his little Purpose in Life.'

'Exactly. And now, do you know what? After all that, I'm feeling a bit peckish. What about you?'

'Starving,' Anna Komarova replied.

She was growing on me by the minute.

Anna Komarova opened the door of the Deserted House, and it suddenly struck me that the place needed a new name. Gold's House. Frankie's House. Or 'the Lived-in House'. Or simply: *Home.*

It would need a bit of thought. But not today. I was wiped out after the roller coaster of emotions that was the past few days. I ate, bumped heads with Anna Komarova by way of thanks, and went upstairs. Climbing into Gold's bed, I could smell him like he was there with me. My good friend Gold. Oh, and by the way, do any of you happen to know what *off limits* means?

19. Last Words

So. That's it. I'd better sign off for now. They tell me every story has to have an end. You can blame humans for that ingenious rule . . . it wasn't my idea.

Of course, I could go on to tell you how I went to Hollywood with Anna Komarova and made a film for *Sauce Supreme*. If you've got a TV, do give it a watch sometime. The Professor and Muscles Nutkin have seen it and think I'm incredibly convincing in the role of Cat Eating Out of Bowl.

But exciting though it was, Hollywood wasn't all it was cracked up to be. The best thing was when I called to see Pussica Purrilenko again. Not only is she strikingly beautiful, but she's a smart one too, you know. Blew me away, she did. Mollies have a habit of doing that to you. Probably not so good for the blood pressure but wonderful all the same.

I went to Linda's grave once and told her that Gold's in the loony bin at the moment, but that he still loves her madly. And that I'll take care of him because she's in heaven and has stuff to do up there. I don't know whether she heard me.

I often mosey along the Big Road, and sometimes I dream that there's a man in the distance coming towards me wearing a dishevelled dressing gown and an old hat, and I'm all ready to bound up to him. But then the dream vanishes into thin air, and I fall back down to earth with a bump, feeling like I'm cursed all over again.

Hey ho. I guess that's the circle of life. You search for a little bit of happiness. You find it. You lose it. And then the whole thing starts all over again. And so on and so forth. But hey, I mustn't grumble. I'm Frankie. You won't hear a bad word about life from me.

About the Authors

J.M. GUTSCH is a reporter at *Der Spiegel* magazine. He has won the Theodor Wolff Prize and the Henri Nannen Prize for his work.

MAXIM LEO was a reporter at the *Berliner Zeitung* for many years. His work has been awarded both the Theodor Wolff Prize and the European Book Prize.

The books that J.M. Gutsch and Maxim Leo have authored together have conquered international best-seller lists, and their joint stage shows regularly sell out.